A STORYTELLER'S CHOICE

A
STORYTELLER'S
CHOICE

A selection of stories,
with notes on how to tell them by
EILEEN COLWELL

With drawings by
CAROL BARKER

THE BODLEY HEAD
LONDON SYDNEY
TORONTO

For my friend
JOHN MASEFIELD
who believes that
'Lovely stories are as necessary
as pure air'
With grateful affection

This collection © The Bodley Head Ltd 1963
Illustrations © The Bodley Head Ltd 1963
ISBN 0 370 01051 5
Printed and bound in Great Britain for
The Bodley Head Ltd
9 Bow Street, London WC2E 7AL
by Unwin Brothers Limited
The Gresham Press, Old Woking, Surrey
Set in Monotype Goudy Modern
First published 1963
Reprinted 1964, 1966, 1969, 1973

Acknowledgments

Every effort has been made to trace the ownership of the copyright material in this book. It is the publishers' belief that the necessary permissions from publishers, authors and authorised agents have been obtained, but in the event of any questions arising as to the use of any material, the publishers, while expressing regret for any error unconsciously made, will be pleased to make the necessary correction in future editions of this book.

Thanks are due to the following for permission to reprint copyright material: The late Miss Eleanor Farjeon for 'Elsie Piddock Skips in her Sleep' from *Martin Pippin in the Daisy Field*, published by Hamish Hamilton Limited, London, and J. B. Lippincott Co., Philadelphia; Routledge and Kegan Paul, London, and Laurence Pollinger Limited for 'The Swallow and the Mole' from *The Long Grass Whispers* by Geraldine Elliot; Jonathan Cape Limited, London, for 'A Chinese Fairy Tale' from *Moonshine and Clover* by Laurence Housman, and for 'Suppose You Met a Witch' from *Belinda and the Swans* by Ian Serraillier; Faber & Faber Limited, London, for 'The Young Man with Music in his Fingers' from *The Wild Cherry* by Diana Ross; David McKay Company Inc., New York, for 'The Jolly Tailor who Became King' from *The Jolly Tailor and Other Fairy Tales translated from the Polish* by Lucia Merecka Borski and Kate B. Miller, © 1928, renewed 1956 by Lucia Merecka Borski and John P. Miller; The author and Methuen and Co. Limited, London, for 'The Monster Who Grew Small' from *The Scarlet Fish and Other Stories* by Joan Grant; The Oxford University Press, London, for 'Where Love Is, God Is' from Tolstoy's *Twenty-Three*

Tales, translated by Aylmer Maude; The Rhoda Power Copyright Trust for 'The Magic Tea-Kettle' from *Stories from Everywhere* by Rhoda Power, published by Evans Bros. Limited, London; The Society of Authors as the Literary Representatives of Dr John Masefield for the extract from *The Midnight Folk*, published by Heinemann Limited, London, reprinted with permission of the Macmillan Company, New York, Copyright 1927 by John Masefield; The Cresset Press, London, for 'A Meal with a Magician' from *My Friend Mr Leakey* by J. B. S. Haldane; George G. Harrap & Co. Limited, London, for 'The Ballad of Semmer-water' from *The Poems of Sir William Watson 1878–1935*; Miss Rumer Godden for *The Mousewife*, published by Macmillan & Co. Limited, London, and The Viking Press Inc., New York; Henry Z. Walck Inc., New York, for *The Hurdy-Gurdy Man* by Margery W. Bianco; Mervyn Skipper for 'Lazy Tok' from *The Meeting Pool*; and The Executors of the Estate of the late Marie Shedlock for her translation of 'The Nightingale' by Hans Andersen from *The Art of the Storyteller*, Copyright 1915 by D. Appleton & Co., Copyright 1936 by D. Appleton-Century Inc., New York.

The verse on page 11 comes from *Listen* by Walter de la Mare, and is reprinted by permission of The Literary Trustees of Walter de la Mare and the Society of Authors as their representative.

CONTENTS

Preface

From the earliest days of history, men have told stories and through them kept alive the deeds of mighty heroes and explained natural wonders. The position of the storyteller used to be an honourable one and, in the Middle Ages, he could demand as his due a harp from the King and a ring from the Queen. Listening to tales was the favourite pastime of the people and for centuries the professional storyteller gave pleasure to untold multitudes. Gradually the status of the storyteller declined, until today storytelling is no longer a living art and the old tales, handed down orally for so many centuries, have become the preserve of the scholar.

Yet children still love to listen to stories the world over, and I believe that they need them from infancy. Because I feel this so deeply, I have told stories as often and in as many places as possible. Storytelling not only gives delight, but there can be no better way of introducing literature to children and of encouraging them to listen to the music of words.

I have *told* stories always, not read them. For both the audience and the storyteller this is more enjoyable and memorable. The children receive the story as a living experience, the storyteller is helped and stimulated by the response of the listeners. All the stories in this book have been shared with children in this way.

There are two essentials in choosing stories to tell. Firstly the story, if it is to be told with enthusiasm and sincerity, must appeal strongly to the storyteller himself. Secondly it must be remembered that the story that reads well, does not necessarily tell well. For this reason I have reluctantly omitted Walter de la Mare's beautiful stories from this collection, for he is essentially a contemplative and descriptive poet. To abridge his stories sufficiently for telling would demand such skill and perception, that I hesitate to suggest it.

Let no one imagine that storytelling is easy. There is no short cut to perfection. Much reading must be done before the right story is found; much preparation is needed for the story to be so thoroughly absorbed that it can be told effort-lessly and freely. But at last the time comes when we are able to say with Walter de la Mare:—

> 'Quiet your faces; be crossed every thumb;
> Fix on me deep your eyes;
> And out of my mind a story shall come,
> Old, and lovely, and wise.'

As we see the expectancy on our children's faces and know that we have a story worthy of that eager anticipation, we have our reward.

EILEEN COLWELL

Elsie Piddock Skips in her Sleep

Elsie Piddock lived in Glynde under Caburn, where lots of
other little girls lived too. They lived mostly on bread-and-
butter, because their mothers were too poor to buy cake. As
soon as Elsie began to hear, she heard the other little girls
skipping every evening after school in the lane outside her
mother's cottage. Swish-swish! went the rope through the
air. Tappity-tap! went the little girls' feet on the ground.
Mumble-umble-umble! went the children's voices, saying a
rhyme that the skipper could skip to. In course of time,
Elsie not only heard the sounds, but understood what they
were all about, and then the mumble-umble turned itself into
words like this:

> 'ANdy SPANdy SUGARdy CANdy,
>   FRENCH ALmond ROCK!
> Breadandbutterforyoursupper'sallyourmother'sGOT!'

The second bit went twice as fast as the first bit, and when
the little girls said it Elsie Piddock, munching her supper,

always munched her mouthful of bread-and-butter in double-quick time. She wished she had some Sugardy-Candy-French-Almond-Rock to suck during the first bit, but she never had.

When Elsie Piddock was three years old, she asked her mother for a skipping-rope.

'You're too little,' said her mother. 'Bide a bit till you're a bigger girl, then you shall have one.'

Elsie pouted and said no more. But in the middle of the night her parents were wakened by something going Slap-slap! on the floor, and there was Elsie in her night-gown skipping with her father's braces. She skipped till her feet caught in the tail of them, and she tumbled down and cried. But she had skipped ten times running first.

'Bless my buttons, mother!' said Mr Piddock. 'The child's a born skipper.'

And Mrs Piddock jumped out of bed full of pride, rubbed Elsie's elbows for her, and said: 'There-a-there now! dry your tears, and tomorrow you shall have a skip-rope all of your own.'

So Elsie dried her eyes on the hem of her night-gown; and in the morning, before he went to work, Mr Piddock got a little cord, just the right length, and made two little wooden handles to go on the ends. With this Elsie skipped all day, scarcely stopping to eat her breakfast of bread-and-butter, and her dinner of butter-and-bread. And in the evening, when the schoolchildren were gathered in the lane, Elsie went out among them, and began to skip with the best.

'Oh!' cried Joan Challon, who was the champion skipper of them all, 'just look at little Elsie Piddock skipping as never so!'

All the skippers stopped to look, and then to wonder. Elsie Piddock certainly *did* skip as never so, and they called to their mothers to come and see. And the mothers in the lane came to their doors, and threw up their hands, and cried: 'Little Elsie Piddock is a born skipper!'

By the time she was five she could outskip any of them:
whether in 'Andy Spandy', 'Lady, Lady, drop your Purse',
'Charley Parley stole some Barley', or whichever of the
games it might be. By the time she was six her name and
fame were known to all the villages in the county. And by
the time she was seven, the fairies heard of her. They were
fond of skipping themselves, and they had a special Skipping-
Master who taught them new skips every month at the new
moon. As they skipped they chanted:

> 'The High Skip,
> The Sly Skip,
> The Skip like a Feather,
> The Long Skip,
> The Strong Skip,
> And the Skip All Together!

> 'The Slow Skip,
> The Toe Skip,
> The Skip Double-Double,
> The Fast Skip,
> The Last Skip,
> And the Skip against Trouble!'

All these skips had their own meanings, and were made
up by the Skipping-Master, whose name was Andy-Spandy.
He was very proud of his fairies, because they skipped better
than the fairies of any other county; but he was also very
severe with them if they did not please him. One night he
scolded Fairy Heels-o'-Lead for skipping badly, and praised
Fairy Flea-Foot for skipping well. Then Fairy Heels-o'-Lead
sniffed and snuffed, and said: 'Hhm-hhm-hhm! there's a
little girl in Glynde who could skip Flea-Foot round the
moon and back again. A born skipper she is, and she skips
as never so.'

'What is her name?' asked Andy-Spandy.

'Her name is Elsie Piddock, and she has skipped down every village far and near, from Didling to Wannock.'

'Go and fetch her here!' commanded Andy-Spandy.

Off went Heels-o'-Lead, and poked her head through Elsie's little window under the eaves, crying: 'Elsie Piddock! Elsie Piddock! there's a Skipping-Match on Caburn, and Fairy Flea-Foot says she can skip better than you.'

Elsie Piddock was fast asleep, but the words got into her dream, so she hopped out of bed with her eyes closed, took her skipping-rope, and followed Heels-o'-Lead to the top of Mount Caburn, where Andy-Spandy and the fairies were waiting for them.

'Skip, Elsie Piddock!' said Andy-Spandy, 'and show us what you're worth!'

Elsie twirled her rope and skipped in her sleep, and as she skipped she murmured:

'ANdy SPANdy SUGARdy CANdy,
FRENCH ALmond ROCK!
Breadandbutterforyoursupper'sallyourmother'sGOT!'

Andy-Spandy watched her skipping with his eyes as sharp as needles, but he could find no fault with it, nor could the fairies.

'Very good, as far as it goes!' said Andy-Spandy. 'Now let us see how far it *does* go. Stand forth, Elsie and Flea-Foot, for the Long Skip.'

Elsie had never done the Long Skip, and if she had had all her wits about her she wouldn't have known what Andy-Spandy meant; but as she was dreaming, she understood him perfectly. So she twirled her rope, and as it came over jumped as far along the ground as she could, about twelve feet from where she had started. Then Flea-Foot did the Long Skip, and skipped clean out of sight.

'Hum!' said Andy-Spandy. 'Now, Elsie Piddock, let us see you do the Strong Skip.'

Once more Elsie understood what was wanted of her; she put both feet together, jumped her rope, and came down with all her strength, so that her heels sank into the ground. Then Flea-Foot did the Strong Skip, and sank into the ground as deep as her waist.

'Hum!' said Andy-Spandy. 'And now, Elsie Piddock, let us see you do the Skip All Together.'

At his words, all the fairies leaped to their ropes, and began skipping as lively as they could, and Elsie with them. An hour went by, two hours, and three hours; one by one the fairies fell down exhausted, and Elsie Piddock skipped on. Just before morning she was skipping all by herself.

Then Andy-Spandy wagged his head and said: 'Elsie Piddock, you are a born skipper. There's no tiring you at all. And for that you shall come once a month to Caburn when the moon is new, and I will teach you to skip till a year is up. And after that I'll wager there won't be mortal or fairy to touch you.'

Andy-Spandy was as good as his word. Twelve times during the next year Elsie Piddock rose up in her sleep with the new moon, and went to the top of Mount Caburn. There she took her place among the fairies, and learned to do all the tricks of the skipping-rope, until she did them better than any. At the end of the year she did the High Skip so well, that she skipped right over the moon.

In the Sly Skip not a fairy could catch her, or know where she would skip to next; so artful was she, that she could skip through the lattice of a skeleton leaf, and never break it.

She redoubled the Skip Double-Double, in which you only had to double yourself up twice round the skipping-rope before it came down. Elsie Piddock did it four times.

In the Fast Skip, she skipped so fast that you couldn't see her, though she stood on the same spot all the time.

In the Last Skip, when all the fairies skipped over the same rope in turn, running round and round till they made a mistake from giddiness, Elsie never got giddy, and never made a mistake, and was always left in last.

In the Slow Skip, she skipped so slow that a mole had time to throw up his hill under her rope before she came down.

In the Toe Skip, when all the others skipped on their tiptoes, Elsie never touched a grass-blade with more than the edge of her toe-nail.

In the Skip Against Trouble, she skipped so joyously that Andy-Spandy himself chuckled with delight.

In the Long Skip she skipped from Caburn to the other end of Sussex, and had to be fetched back by the wind.

In the Strong Skip, she went right under the earth, as a diver goes under the sea, and the rabbits, whose burrows she had disturbed, handed her up again.

But in the Skip like a Feather she came down like gossamer, so that she could alight on a spider-thread and never shake the dew-drop off.

And in the Skip All Together, she could skip down the whole tribe of fairies, and remain as fresh as a daisy. Nobody had ever found out how long Elsie Piddock could skip without getting tired, for everybody else got tired first. Even Andy-Spandy didn't know.

At the end of the year he said to her: 'Elsie Piddock, I have taught you all. Bring me your skipping-rope, and you shall have a prize.'

Elsie gave her rope to Andy-Spandy, and he licked the two little wooden handles, first the one and then the other. When he handed the rope back to her, one of the handles was made of Sugar Candy, and the other of French Almond Rock.

'There!' said Andy-Spandy. 'Though you suck them never so, they will never grow less, and you shall therefore suck sweet all your life. And as long as you are little enough to skip with this rope, you shall skip as I have taught you. But when you are too big for this rope, and must get a new one, you will no longer be able to do all the fairy skips that you have learned, although you will still skip better in the mortal way than any other girl that ever was born. Good-bye, Elsie Piddock.'

'Aren't I ever going to skip for you again?' asked Elsie Piddock in her sleep.

But Andy-Spandy didn't answer. For morning had come over the Downs, and the fairies disappeared, and Elsie Piddock went back to bed.

If Elsie had been famous for her skipping before this fairy year, you can imagine what she became after it. She created so much wonder, that she hardly dared to show all she could do. Nevertheless, for another year she did such incredible things, that people came from far and near to see her skip over the church spire, or through the split oak-tree in the Lord's Park, or across the river at its widest point. When there was trouble in her mother's house, or in any house in the village, Elsie Piddock skipped so gaily that the trouble was forgotten in laughter. And when she skipped all the old games in Glynde, along with the little girls, and they sang:

'ANdy SPANdy SUGARdy CANdy,
FRENCH ALmond ROCK !
Breadandbutterforyoursupper'sallyourmother'sGOT!'—

Elsie Piddock said: 'It aren't all *I've* got!' and gave them a suck of her skipping-rope handles all round. And on the night of the new moon, she always led the children up Mount Caburn, where she skipped more marvellously than ever. In fact, it was Elsie Piddock who established the custom of New-Moon-Skipping on Caburn.

But at the end of another year she had grown too big to skip with her little rope. She laid it away in a box, and went on skipping with a longer one. She still skipped as never so, but her fairy tricks were laid by with the rope, and though her friends teased her to do the marvellous things she used to do, Elsie Piddock only laughed, and shook her head, and never told why. In time, when she was still the pride and wonder of her village, people would say: 'Ah, but you should ha' seen her when she was a littling! Why, she could skip through her mother's keyhole!' And in more time, these stories became a legend that nobody believed. And in still more time, Elsie grew up (though never very much), and became a little woman, and gave up skipping, because skipping-time was over. After fifty years or so, nobody remembered that she had ever skipped at all. Only Elsie knew. For when times were hard, and they often were, she sat by the hearth with her dry crust and no butter, and sucked the Sugar Candy that Andy-Spandy had given her for life.

*   *   *

It was ever and ever so long afterwards. Three new Lords had walked in the Park since the day when Elsie Piddock had skipped through the split oak. Changes had come in the village; old families had died out, new families had arrived; others had moved away to distant parts, the Piddocks among them. Farms had changed hands, cottages had been pulled down, and new ones had been built. But Mount Caburn was as it always had been, and as the people came to think it always would be. And still the children kept the custom of going there each new moon to skip. Nobody remembered how this custom had come about, it was too far back in the years. But customs are customs, and the child who could not skip the new moon in on Caburn stayed at home and cried.

Then a new Lord came to the Park; one not born a Lord, who had grown rich in trade, and bought the old estate. Soon after his coming, changes began to take place more violent than the pulling down of cottages. The new Lord began to

shut up footpaths and destroy rights of way. He stole the
Common rights here and there, as he could. In his greed for
more than he had got, he raised rents and pressed the people
harder than they could bear. But bad as the high rents were
to them, they did not mind these so much as the loss of their
old rights. They fought the new Lord, trying to keep what
had been theirs for centuries, and sometimes they won the
fight, but oftener lost it. The constant quarrels bred a spirit
of anger between them and the Lord, and out of hate he was
prepared to do whatever he could to spite them.

Amongst the lands over which he exercised a certain power
was Caburn. This had been always open to the people, and
the Lord determined if he could to close it. Looking up the
old deeds, he discovered that, though the Down was his, he
was obliged to leave a way upon it by which the people could
go from one village to another. For hundreds of years they
had made a short cut of it over the top.

The Lord's Lawyer told him that, by the wording of the
deeds, he could never stop the people from travelling by way
of the Downs.

'Can't I!' snorted the Lord. 'Then at least I will make
them travel a long way round!'

And he had plans drawn up to enclose the whole of the
top of Caburn, so that nobody could walk on it. This meant
that the people must trudge miles round the base, as they
passed from place to place. The Lord gave out that he needed
Mount Caburn to build great factories on.

The village was up in arms to defend its rights.

'Can he do it?' they asked those who knew; and they
were told: 'It is not quite certain, but we fear he can.' The
Lord himself was not quite certain either but he went on
with his plans, and each new move was watched with anger
and anxiety by the villagers. And not only by the villagers;
for the fairies saw that their own skipping-ground was
threatened. How could they ever skip there again when the

grass was turned to cinders, and the new moon blackened by chimney-smoke?

The Lawyer said to the Lord: 'The people will fight you tooth and nail.'

'Let 'em!' blustered the Lord; and he asked uneasily: 'Have they a leg to stand on?'

'Just half a leg,' said the Lawyer. 'It would be as well not to begin building yet, and if you can come to terms with them you'd better.'

The Lord sent word to the villagers that, though he undoubtedly could do what he pleased, he would, out of his good heart, restore to them a footpath he had blocked, if they would give up all pretensions to Caburn.

'Footpath, indeed!' cried stout John Maltman, among his cronies at the Inn. 'What's a footpath to Caburn? Why, our mothers skipped there as children, and our children skip there now. And we hope to see our children's children skip there. If Caburn top be built over, 'twill fair break my little Ellen's heart.'

'Ay, and my Margery's,' said another.

'And my Mary's and Kitty's!' cried a third. Others spoke up, for nearly all had daughters whose joy it was to skip on Caburn at the new moon.

John Maltman turned to their best adviser, who had studied the matter closely, and asked: 'What think ye? Have we a leg to stand on?'

'Only half a one,' said the other. 'I doubt if you can stop him. It might be as well to come to terms.'

'None of his footpaths for us,' swore stout John Maltman. 'We'll fight the matter out.'

So things were left for a little, and each side wondered what the next move would be. Only the people knew in their hearts that they must be beaten in the end and the Lord was sure of his victory. So sure, that he had great loads of bricks ordered; but he did not begin building for fear the people might grow violent, and perhaps burn his ricks and destroy his property. The only thing he did was to put a wire fence round the top of Caburn, and set a keeper there to send the people round it. The people broke the fence in many places, and jumped it, and crawled under it; and as the keeper could not be everywhere at once, many of them crossed the Down almost under his nose.

One evening, just before the new moon was due, Ellen Maltman went into the woods to cry. For she was the best skipper under Mount Caburn, and the thought that she would never skip there again made her more unhappy than she had ever thought she could be. While she was crying in the dark, she felt a hand on her shoulder, and a voice said to her: 'Crying for trouble, my dear? That'll never do!'

The voice might have been the voice of a withered leaf, it was so light and dry; but it was also kind, so Ellen checked her sobs and said: 'It's a big trouble, ma'am, there's no remedy against it *but* to cry.'

'Why, yes, there is,' said the withered voice. 'Ye should skip against trouble, my dear.'

At this Ellen's sobs burst forth anew. 'I'll never skip no more!' she wailed. 'If I can't skip the new moon in on Caburn, I'll never skip no more.'

'And why can't you skip the new moon in on Caburn?' asked the voice.

Then Ellen told her.

After a little pause the voice spoke quietly out of the darkness. 'It's more than you will break their hearts if they cannot skip on Caburn. And it must not be, it must not be. Tell me your name.'

'Ellen Maltman, ma'am, and I do love skipping. I can skip down anybody, ma'am, and they say I skip as never so!'

'They do, do they?' said the withered voice. 'Well, Ellen, run you home and tell them this. They are to go to this Lord and tell him he shall have his way and build on Caburn, if

he will first take down the fence and let all who have ever
skipped there skip there once more by turns, at the new moon.
All, mind you, Ellen. And when the last skipper skips the
last skip, he may lay his first brick. And let it be written out
on paper, and signed and sealed.'

'But ma'am!' said Ellen, wondering.

'No words, child. Do as I tell you.' And the withered
voice sounded so compelling that Ellen resisted no more. She
ran straight to the village, and told her story to everybody.

At first they could hardly swallow it; and even when they
had swallowed it, they said: 'But what's the sense of it?'
But Ellen persisted and persisted; something of the spirit of
the old voice got into her words, and against their reason
the people began to think it was the thing to do. To cut a
long story short they sent the message to the Lord next
day.

The Lord could scarcely believe his ears. He rubbed his
hands, and chortled at the people for fools.

'They've come to terms!' he sneered. 'I shall have the
Down, and keep my footpath too. Well, they shall have their
Skipping-Party; and the moment it is ended, up go my
factories!'

The paper was drawn out, signed by both parties in the
presence of witnesses, and duly sealed; and on the night of
the new moon, the Lord invited a party of his friends to go
with him to Caburn to see the sight.

And what a sight it was for them to see; every little girl in
the village was there with her skipping-rope, from the
toddlers to those who had just turned up their hair. Nay,
even the grown maidens and the young mothers were there;
and the very matrons too had come with ropes. Had not they
once as children skipped on Caburn? And the message had
said 'All.' Yes, and others were there, others they could not
see: Andy-Spandy and his fairy team, Heels-o'Lead, Flea-Foot,
and all of the rest, were gathered round to watch with

bright fierce eyes the last great skipping on their precious ground.

The skipping began. The toddlers first, a skip or so apiece, a stumble, and they fell out. The Lord and his party laughed aloud at the comical mites, and at another time the villagers would have laughed too. But there was no laughter in them tonight. Their eyes were bright and fierce like those of the fairies. After the toddlers the little girls skipped in the order of their ages, and as they got older, the skipping got better. In the thick of the schoolchildren, 'This will take some time,' said the Lord impatiently. And when Ellen Maltman's turn came, and she went into her thousands, he grew restive. But even she, who could skip as never so, tired at last; her foot tripped, and she fell on the ground with a little sob. None lasted even half her time; of those who followed some were better, some were worse, than others; and in the small hours the older women were beginning to take their turn. Few of them kept it up for half a minute; they hopped and puffed bravely, but their skipping days were done. As they had laughed at the babies, so now the Lord's friends jibed at the babies' grandmothers.

'Soon over now,' said the Lord, as the oldest of the women who had come to skip, a fat old dame of sixty-seven, stepped out and twirled her rope. Her foot caught in it; she staggered, dropped the rope, and hid her face in her hands.

'Done!' shouted the Lord; and he brandished at the crowd a trowel and a brick which he had brought with him. 'Clear out, the lot of you! I am going to lay the first brick. The skipping's ended!'

'No, if you please,' said a gentle withered voice, 'it is my turn now.' And out of the crowd stepped a tiny tiny woman, so very old, so very bent and fragile, that she seemed to be no bigger than a little child.

'You!' cried the Lord. 'Who are *you*?'

'My name is Elsie Piddock, if you please, and I am a

hundred and nine years old. For the last seventy-nine years I
have lived over the border, but I was born in Glynde, and I
skipped on Caburn as a child.' She spoke like one in a dream,
and her eyes were closed.

'Elsie Piddock! Elsie Piddock!' the name ran in a whisper
round the crowd.

'Elsie Piddock!' murmured Ellen Maltman. 'Why, mum,
I thought Elsie Piddock was just a tale.'

'Nay, Elsie Piddock was no tale!' said the fat woman who
had skipped last. 'My mother Joan skipped with her many a
time, and told me tales you never would believe.'

'Elsie Piddock!' they all breathed again; and a wind
seemed to fly round Mount Caburn, shrilling the name with
glee. But it was no wind, it was Andy-Spandy and his fairy
team, for they had seen the skipping-rope in the tiny woman's
hands. One of the handles was made of Sugar Candy, and the
other was made of French Almond Rock.

But the new Lord had never even heard of Elsie Piddock as
a story; so laughing coarsely once again, he said: 'One more
bump for an old woman's bones! Skip, Elsie Piddock, and
show us what you're worth.'

'Yes, skip, Elsie Piddock,' cried Andy-Spandy and the
fairies, 'and show them what you're worth!'

Then Elsie Piddock stepped into the middle of the on-
lookers, twirled her baby rope over her little shrunken body,
and began to skip. And she skipped as NEVER so!

First of all she skipped:

'ANdy SPANdy SUGARdy CANdy,
    FRENCH ALmond ROCK!
Breadandbutterforyoursupper'sallyourmother'sGOT!'

And nobody could find fault with her skipping. Even the
Lord gasped: 'Wonderful! wonderful for an old woman!'
But Ellen Maltman, who *knew*, whispered: 'Oh, mum! 'tis

wonderful for *any*body! And oh mum, do but see—she's
skipping in her sleep!'

It was true. Elsie Piddock, shrunk to the size of seven
years old, was sound asleep, skipping the new moon in with
her baby rope that was up to all the tricks. An hour went
by, two hours, three hours. There was no stopping her, and
no tiring her. The people gasped, the Lord fumed, and the
fairies turned head-over-heels for joy. When morning broke
the Lord cried: 'That's enough!'

But Elsie Piddock went on skipping.

'Time's up!' cried the Lord.

'When I skip my last skip, you shall lay your first brick,'
said Elsie Piddock.

The villagers broke into a cheer.

'Signed and sealed, my lord, signed and sealed,' said Elsie
Piddock.

'But hang it, old woman, you can't go on for ever!' cried
the Lord.

'Oh yes, I can,' said Elsie Piddock. And on she went.

At midday the Lord shouted: 'Will the woman never
stop?'

'No, she won't,' said Elsie Piddock. And she didn't.

'Then I'll stop you!' stormed the Lord, and made a grab
at her.

'Now for a Sly Skip,' said Elsie Piddock, and skipped
right through his thumb and forefinger.

'Hold her, you!' yelled the Lord to his Lawyer.

'Now for a High Skip,' said Elsie Piddock, and as the
Lawyer darted at her, she skipped right over the highest
lark singing in the sun.

The villagers shouted for glee, and the Lord and his
friends were furious. Forgotten was the compact signed and
sealed—their one thought now was to seize the maddening
old woman, and stop her skipping by sheer force. But they
couldn't. She played all her tricks on them: High Skip, Slow

Skip, Sly Skip, Toe Skip, Long Skip, Fast Skip, Strong Skip,
but never Last Skip. On and on and on she went. When the
sun began to set, she was still skipping.

'Can we never rid the Down of the old thing?' cried the
Lord desperately.

'No,' answered Elsie Piddock in her sleep, 'the Down will
never be rid of me more. It's the children of Glynde I'm
skipping for, to hold the Down for them and theirs for ever;
it's Andy-Spandy I'm skipping for once again, for through
him I've sucked sweet all my life. Oh, Andy, even you never
knew how long Elsie Piddock could go on skipping!'

'The woman's mad!' cried the Lord. 'Signed and sealed
doesn't hold with a madwoman. Skip or no skip, I shall lay
the first brick!'

He plunged his trowel into the ground, and forced his
brick down into the hole as a token of his possession of the
land.

'Now,' said Elsie Piddock, 'for a Strong Skip!'

Right on the top of the brick she skipped, and down under-
ground she sank out of sight, bearing the brick beneath her.
Wild with rage, the Lord dived after her. Up came Elsie
Piddock skipping blither than ever—but the Lord never came
up again. The Lawyer ran to look down the hole; but there
was no sign of him. The Lawyer reached his arm down the
hole; but there was no reaching him. The Lawyer dropped a
pebble down the hole; and no one heard it fall. So strong had
Elsie Piddock skipped the Strong Skip.

The Lawyer shrugged his shoulders, and he and the Lord's
friends left Mount Caburn for good and all. Oh, how joyously
Elsie Piddock skipped then!

'Skip Against Trouble!' cried she, and skipped so that
everyone present burst into happy laughter. To the tune of
it she skipped the Long Skip, clean out of sight. And the
people went home to tea. Caburn was saved for their children,
and for the fairies, for ever.

But that wasn't the end of Elsie Piddock; she has never stopped skipping on Caburn since, for Signed and Sealed is Signed and Sealed. Not many have seen her, because she knows all the tricks; but if you go to Caburn at the new moon, you may catch a glimpse of a tiny bent figure, no bigger than a child, skipping all by itself in its sleep, and hear a gay little voice, like the voice of a dancing yellow leaf, singing:

'*ANdy SPANdy SUGARdy CANdy,*
FRENCH ALmond ROCK!
Breadandbutterforyoursupper'sallyourmother'sGOT!'

From *Martin Pippin in the Daisy Field* by Eleanor Farjeon (Hamish Hamilton Limited, London, and Lippincott, Philadelphia and N.Y.)

(See Note, page 209)

The Swallow and the Mole

Mfuko, the Mole, twitched a sensitive ear, cocked his head on one side and listened intently. Undoubtedly something had fallen on the ground above him—something that seemed to be making pitiful little moaning noises.

'Better go and see what it is,' said Mfuko to himself. 'May be someone in need of help.'

He tunnelled rapidly to the surface and thrust a cautious head through the soft earth. At first he could see nothing, for the bright sunlight made him blink, and his eyesight was never good. But his keen hearing directed him to the moaning sounds and by the time he reached the place they came from he could just make out the form of a small bird lying, apparently exhausted, on the ground.

'My poor fellow,' exclaimed Mole in great concern. 'What has happened? Is anything broken?'

'I don't know,' replied the bird, speaking with difficulty. 'I fell . . . so tired . . . been flying for days . . . O-oh!' he sighed, and closed his weary eyes.

'There, there!' said Mole. 'Don't you talk any more. Just rest quietly here while I go and fetch some food and water for you. I expect that's what you need!' And Mfuko bustled off to his own store as fast as he could. Luckily his water-pot was full, so there was no difficulty about that, but food? . . . the only food he had was Worm, and surely all birds ate 'Worm'? If not he'd have to find something else! Mole hurried back.

'Now,' he said, 'a drink of water'll do you good. And then, what about a nice fat Worm?'

The bird's eyes opened and he nodded feebly, but made no

attempt to move, so Mole splashed a little water over him. This helped to revive him, and, with an effort, the bird struggled to his feet and started to drink. He drank and he drank and he drank, and when at last he had had enough he turned to the Mole.

'*Did* you say "Worm"?' he asked.

Mfuko nodded and produced what had been the finest Worm in the larder.

'How kind,' murmured the bird and gobbled it up. 'I suppose you haven't any more?'

'Yes, certainly. Here you are. Help yourself and have as many as you like.'

'Thank you, thank you,' said the bird gratefully and swallowed three in quick succession. 'Mm . . . delicious! I feel quite different now. I really don't know how I can ever repay you for your kindness.'

'That's all right,' said Mole hastily. 'Only too glad to have been of use.'

'Hullo! Hullo!' a voice called out suddenly. 'What's happening here?'

Mole looked round to see who the newcomer might be.

'Why, it's my old friend Kamba!' he exclaimed delightedly. Then he turned to the bird and said: 'You must meet my friend, the Tortoise. I'll introduce you. What, if I may ask, is your name?'

'Namazeze. I am Namazeze, the Swallow.'

'And what has brought you to these parts?' asked Kamba when the introductions had been made.

'Chance,' replied the Swallow, and began to tell them of his great flight. Spellbound they listened to the tale; from the far North he had come, he and all his friends and relations—but a great storm had arisen and somehow he had become separated from the others.

'Oh!' exclaimed Kamba suddenly, as Swallow was pausing

for breath. 'I'd quite forgotten the reason of my visit to-day!
I came to tell you about the competition.'

'What competition?' asked Mole.

'You know—the yearly one for the election of the Chief.'

'What is it to be this time?'

'A sort of ball game. Njobvu, the Elephant, is to throw the
ball high into the air and whoever catches it will be elected
Chief.'

'Hm!' said Mole. 'And, of course, Elephant will be the
one to catch the ball. It is easy for him with that long trunk
of his! I don't want to be unkind,' he continued, 'but I do
think it is rather . . . er . . . well . . . noticeable the way
Elephant always chooses a competition that he is certain
of winning, don't you?'

'Yes,' agreed Kamba. 'It certainly is very noticeable.
Really, it hardly seems worth our while to compete, but I
suppose we must—for the look of the thing. I do wish someone
else *could* win this time!'

'When is the competition to take place?' asked the
Swallow suddenly.

'In two days' time. Why?'

'Oh, I just wondered.'

'I think I ought to be going now,' said Kamba. 'I'll see
you at the competition, Mfuko, if not before. Will you be
there, Namazeze?'

'Perhaps,' answered the Swallow, thoughtfully. 'It might
be rather interesting.'

On the morning of the competition Mfuko, the Mole,
emerged from his home, looking very spruce, and carrying a
large bag made of civet-skin. He was exceedingly proud of this
bag, which had belonged to his great-grandfather, and he
always took it with him whenever he went anywhere
important.

Namazeze, the Swallow, was waiting for him, and together they walked towards the place where the competition was to be held. Just as they were getting near, Swallow suddenly stopped and said he felt dreadfully tired.

'I suppose you couldn't manage to carry me in that bag of yours?' he asked the Mole. 'I don't weigh much, and I do so want to come with you.'

'Of course,' said Mole instantly. 'In you get! You'll be quite comfortable and you'll find a Worm or two in there, if you should feel hungry.'

'*How* kind you are,' murmured Namazeze as he climbed in. 'You'll leave the bag open a little so that I can breathe, won't you?' he added. 'And don't say anything to anybody about my being here. I'd rather no one knew.'

'Just as you like, my dear fellow,' said Mole and, grasping the bag firmly, he hurried on.

All the animals for miles round had gathered in the wide, open space where the competition was about to take place. It was a hot day and very dusty, and by the time Mfuko arrived he was only too glad to put his bag on the ground and sit down beside it. He peered round for a while, but what with the glare and the dust and his own bad sight, he could not see any of his particular friends, though he could hear Njobvu, the Elephant, explaining about the ball game to those who were crowding round him. Mole didn't think it worth while to pay much attention to what was being said—after all, what chance had a little creature like himself? Why, he'd never even see the ball, let alone catch it!

Suddenly Elephant trumpeted loudly.

'Do you all understand?' he shouted. 'The person who catches this ball will be the new Chief. Now, are you ready? . . . Are you ready? . . . Go!' And he threw the ball (a green bush-orange) high into the air.

Up it went and up, and all the animals jostled and pushed and craned their necks to watch it, but they made so much

dust that they could not see a thing. Certainly they could not
see Namazeze, the Swallow, fly out of Mole's little bag, nor
did they see him catch the ball in mid-air and come flying
back again. And all that Mole himself saw was a large, green
ball descending right into his paws.

'Where is the ball?' cried all the animals. 'Has no one
caught it?'

'Yes, I have,' said Mole in a small, surprised voice.

'You? Mole? Impossible!' Everyone was amazed.

'Yes, here it is,' said Mole, and ran forward with the ball.

For a moment there was silence. Then Njobvu spoke with
scarcely-veiled annoyance.

'Well done, Mfuko,' he said. 'But, of course, the ball has
to be caught *three* times.'

'Oh!' Mole felt rather crushed and disappointed, and
returned sadly to his bag. As he reached it he peeped inside
to see if Namazeze was all right. Yes, there the Swallow was,
apparently fast asleep. Mole sat down and waited for the
ball to be thrown a second time.

'Are you all ready?' shouted Njobvu a moment later. 'Are
you ready? Go!'

Up went the ball again, the animals pushed and jostled,
the dust grew thicker and thicker, and out flew the Swallow,
unnoticed by anyone, and when the animals cried: 'Where is
the ball? Who has it?' Mole was as amazed as everyone else
to find that it was clasped firmly in his own two paws.

'Well!' he thought to himself. 'This really is most extra-
ordinary!' and, shaking his head in a rather bewildered way,
he ran and gave the ball back to the Elephant.

Njobvu scowled at him and said nothing, and Mfuko returned to his place by the bag. He was beginning to feel very
excited and listened eagerly for the next 'Are you ready?
Go!'

For the third time the ball went up. Up . . . up . . . and
up. Again the animals pushed and jostled, again they raised

a cloud of dust, again the Swallow flew unnoticed into the air. And for the third time Mfuko, the Mole, suddenly found the ball descending into his own paws. Tightly he clutched it, tightly he held it, and without waiting for the cry of: 'Who has the ball?' he shouted 'I've got it! I've got it,' and he began to dance about with delight.

'Well done!' yelled Kamba, the Tortoise. 'Now you are our Chief. Mfuko is our Chief!' The cry was taken up and echoed by everyone except Njobvu, the Elephant, who was disgusted at the way his plans had failed. But even he had to accept the fact that Mfuko *was* the new Chief, and all the other animals were delighted, for they were sure that Mole would be much better than the Elephant.

On the way home Kamba, who was walking with the proud and happy Mole, enquired after the Swallow.

'I didn't see Namazeze this morning, did you?' he said.

'No, you wouldn't have seen him,' answered Mole. 'The poor fellow was so tired that he asked me to put him in my bag so that he could rest. He didn't want me to tell anyone, but I'm sure he won't mind your knowing.'

'Is he there now?' Kamba asked.

Mole opened the bag a little wider and showed it to the Tortoise.

'Hullo,' said Namazeze sleepily, opening one eye. 'Is the competition over?'

'Yes,' said Kamba. 'And who do you think is the new Chief?'

'Njobvu, the Elephant, I suppose?'

'No. Mole is! He caught the ball! *Three* times!! Isn't it wonderful! What a pity you were asleep.'

Namazeze looked at the Tortoise, and there was an odd expression on his face. Then: 'Yes,' he said carelessly. 'Wasn't it a pity!'

From *The Long Grass Whispers* by Geraldine Elliot (Routledge and Kegan Paul, London, and Dufour, Chester Springs, Pa.)

(See Note, page 210)

A Chinese Fairy Tale

Tiki-Pu was a small grub of a thing; but he had a true love of Art deep down in his soul. There it hung mewing and complaining, struggling to work its way out through the raw exterior that bound it.

Tiki-Pu's master professed to be an artist: he had apprentices and students, who came daily to work under him, and a large studio littered about with the performances of himself and his pupils. On the walls hung also a few real works by the older men, all long since dead.

This studio Tiki-Pu swept; for those who worked in it he ground colours, washed brushes, and ran errands, bringing them their dog chops and bird's nest soup from the nearest eating-house whenever they were too busy to go out for it themselves. He himself had to feed mainly on the breadcrumbs which the students screwed into pellets for their drawings and then threw about on the floor. It was on the floor, also, that he had to sleep at night.

Tiki-Pu looked after the blinds, and mended the windowpanes, which were often broken when the apprentices threw their brushes and mahl-sticks at him. Also he strained ricepaper over the linen-stretchers, ready for the painters to

work on; and for a treat, now and then, a lazy one would
allow him to mix a colour for him. Then it was that Tiki-Pu's
soul came down into his finger-tips, and his heart beat so that
he gasped for joy. Oh, the yellows and the greens, and the
lakes and the cobalts, and the purples which sprang from the
blending of them! Sometimes it was all he could do to keep
himself from crying out.

Tiki-Pu, while he squatted and ground at the colour-
powders, would listen to his master lecturing to the students.
He knew by heart the names of all the painters and their
schools, and the name of the great leader of them all who had
lived and passed from their midst more than three hundred
years ago; he knew that too, a name like the sound of the
wind, Wio-Wani: the big picture at the end of the studio
was by him.

That picture! To Tiki-Pu it seemed worth all the rest of
the world put together. He knew, too, the story which was
told of it, making it as holy to his eyes as the tombs of his
own ancestors. The apprentices joked over it, calling it, 'Wio-
Wani's back-door', 'Wio-Wani's night-cap', and many other
nicknames; but Tiki-Pu was quite sure, since the picture was
so beautiful, that the story must be true.

Wio-Wani, at the end of a long life, had painted it; a
garden full of trees and sunlight, with high-standing flowers
and green paths, and in their midst a palace. 'The place
where I would like to rest,' said Wio-Wani, when it was
finished.

So beautiful was it then, that the Emperor himself had
come to see it; and gazing enviously at those peaceful walks,
and the palace nestling among the trees, had sighed and
owned that he too would be glad of such a resting-place.
Then Wio-Wani stepped into the picture, and walked away
along a path till he came, looking quite small and far-off, to
a low door in the palace wall. Opening it, he turned and
beckoned to the Emperor; but the Emperor did not follow;

so Wio-Wani went in by himself, and shut the door between himself and the world for ever.

That happened three hundred years ago; but for Tiki-Pu the story was as fresh and true as if it had happened yester-day. When he was left to himself in the studio, all alone and locked up for the night, Tiki-Pu used to go and stare at the picture till it was too dark to see, and at the little palace with the door in its wall by which Wio-Wani had disappeared out of life. Then his soul would go down into his finger-tips, and he would knock softly and fearfully at the beautifully painted door, saying, 'Wio-Wani, are you there?'

Little by little in the long-thinking nights, and the slow early mornings when light began to creep back through the papered windows of the studio, Tiki-Pu's soul became too much for him. He who could strain paper, and grind colours, and wash brushes, had everything within reach for be-coming an artist, if it was the will of Fate that he should be one.

He began timidly at first, but in a little while he grew bold. With the first wash of light he was up from his couch on the hard floor and was daubing his soul out on scraps, and odds-and-ends, and stolen pieces of rice-paper.

Before long the short spell of daylight which lay between dawn and the arrival of the apprentices to their work did not suffice him. It took him so long to hide all traces of his doings, to wash out the brushes, and rinse clean the paint-pots he had used, and on the top of that to get the studio swept and dusted, that there was hardly time left him in which to indulge the itching of his fingers.

Driven by necessity, he became a pilferer of candle-ends, picking them from their sockets in the lanterns which the students carried on dark nights. Now and then one of these would remember that, when last used, his lantern had had a candle in it, and would accuse Tiki-Pu of having stolen it. 'It is true,' he would confess, 'I was hungry—I have eaten it.' The lie was so probable, he was believed easily, and was well beaten accordingly. Down in the ragged linings of his coat Tiki-Pu could hear the candle-ends rattling as the buffeting and chastisement fell upon him, and often he trembled lest his hoard should be discovered. But the truth of the matter never leaked out; and at night, as soon as he guessed that all the world outside was in bed, Tiki-Pu would mount one of his candles on a wooden stand and paint by the light of it, blinding himself over the task, till the dawn came and gave him a better and cheaper light to work by.

Tiki-Pu quite hugged himself over the results; he believed he was doing very well. 'If only Wio-Wani were here to teach me,' thought he, 'I would be in the way to becoming a great painter!'

The resolution came to him one night that Wio-Wani *should* teach him. So he took a large piece of rice-paper and strained it, and sitting down opposite 'Wio-Wani's back-door', began painting. He had never set himself so big a task as this; by the dim stumbling light of his candle he strained his eyes nearly blind over the difficulties of it; and at last was almost driven to despair. How the trees stood row behind row, with air and sunlight between, and how the path went in and out, winding its way up to the little door in the palace-wall were mysteries he could not fathom. He peered and peered and dropped tears into his paint-pots; but the secret of the mystery of such painting was far beyond him.

The door in the palace-wall opened; out came a little old man and began walking down the pathway towards him.

The soul of Tiki-Pu gave a sharp leap in his grubby little body. 'That must be Wio-Wani himself and no other!' cried his soul.

Tiki-Pu pulled off his cap and threw himself down on the floor with reverent grovellings. When he dared to look up again Wio-Wani stood over him big and fine; just within the edge of the canvas he stood and reached out a hand.

'Come along with me, Tiki-Pu!' said the great one. 'If you want to know how to paint I will teach you.'

'Oh, Wio-Wani, were you there all the while?' cried Tiki-Pu ecstatically, leaping up and clutching with his smeary little puds the hand which the old man extended to him.

'I was there,' said Wio-Wani, 'looking at you out of my little window. Come along in!'

Tiki-Pu took a heave and swung himself into the picture, and fairly capered when he found his feet among the flowers of Wio-Wani's beautiful garden. Wio-Wani had turned, and was ambling gently back to the door of his palace, beckoning to the small one to follow him; and there stood Tiki-Pu, opening his mouth like a fish to all the wonders that surrounded him. 'Celestiality, may I speak?' he said suddenly.

'Speak,' replied Wio-Wani; 'what is it?'

'The Emperor, was he not the very flower of fools not to follow when you told him?'

'I cannot say,' answered Wio-Wani, 'but he certainly was no artist.'

Then he opened the door, that door which he had so beautifully painted, and led Tiki-Pu in. Outside the little candle-end sat and guttered by itself, till the wick fell overboard, and the flame kicked itself out, leaving the studio in darkness and solitude to wait for the growings of another dawn.

It was full day before Tiki-Pu reappeared; he came running down the green path in great haste, jumped out of the frame on to the studio floor, and began tidying up his own messes of the night and the apprentices' of the previous day. Only just in time did he have things ready by the hour when his master and the others returned to their work.

All that day they kept scratching their left ears, and could not think why; but Tiki-Pu knew, for he was saying over to himself all the things that Wio-Wani, the great

painter, had been saying about them and their precious pro-
ductions. And as he ground their colours for them and washed
their brushes, and filled his famished little body with the
breadcrumbs they threw away, little they guessed from what
an immeasurable distance he looked down upon them all, and
had Wio-Wani's word for it tickling his right ear all the day
long.

Now before long Tiki-Pu's master noticed a change in him;
and though he bullied him, and thrashed him, and did all
that a careful master should do, he could not get the change
out of him. So in a short while he grew suspicious. 'What is
the boy up to?' he wondered. 'I have my eye on him all day:
it must be at night that he gets into mischief.'

It did not take Tiki-Pu's master a night's watching to find
that something surreptitious was certainly going on. When
it was dark he took up his post outside the studio, to see
whether by any chance Tiki-Pu had some way of getting out;
and before long he saw a faint light showing through the
window. So he came and thrust his finger softly through one
of the panes, and put his eye to the hole.

There inside was a candle burning on a stand, and Tiki-Pu
squatting with paint-pots and brush in front of Wio-Wani's
last masterpiece.

'What fine piece of burglary is this?' thought he; 'What
serpent have I been harbouring in my bosom? Is this beast of
a grub of a boy thinking to make himself a painter and cut
me out of my reputation and prosperity?' For even at that
distance he could plainly perceive that the work of this boy
went head and shoulders beyond his, or that of any painter
living.

Presently Wio-Wani opened his door and came down the
path, as was his habit now each night, to call Tiki-Pu to his
lesson. He advanced to the front of the picture and beckoned
for Tiki-Pu to come in with him; and Tiki-Pu's master grew
clammy at the knees as he beheld Tiki-Pu catch hold of

Wio-Wani's hand and jump into the picture, and skip up the green path by Wio-Wani's side, and in through the little door that Wio-Wani had painted so beautifully in the end wall of his palace!

For a time Tiki-Pu's master stood glued to the spot with grief and horror. 'Oh, you deadly little underling! Oh, you poisonous little caretaker, you parasite, you vampire, you fly in amber!' cried he, 'is that where you get your training? Is it there that you dare to go trespassing; into a picture that I purchased for my own pleasure and profit, and not at all for yours? Very soon we will see whom it really belongs to!'

He ripped out the paper of the largest window-pane and pushed his way through into the studio. Then in great haste he took up paint-pot and brush, and sacrilegiously set him-self to work upon Wio-Wani's last masterpiece. In the place of the doorway by which Tiki-Pu had entered he painted a solid brick wall; twice over he painted it, making it two bricks thick; brick by brick he painted it, and mortared every brick to its place. And when he had quite finished, he laughed, and called, 'Good-night, Tiki-Pu!' and went home to be quite happy.

The next day all the apprentices were wondering what had become of Tiki-Pu; but as the master himself said nothing, and as another boy came to act as colour-grinder and brush-washer to the establishment, they very soon forgot all about him.

In the studio the master used to sit at work with his students all about him, and a mind full of ease and content-ment. Now and then he would throw a glance across to the bricked-up doorway of Wio-Wani's palace, and laugh to himself, thinking how well he had served out Tiki-Pu for his treachery and presumption.

One day—it was five years after the disappearance of Tiki-Pu—he was giving his apprentices a lecture on the glories and the beauties and the wonders of Wio-Wani's painting—how nothing for colour could excel, or for mystery could equal it. To add point to his eloquence, he stood waving his hands before Wio-Wani's last masterpiece, and all his students and apprentices sat round him and looked.

Suddenly he stopped at mid-word, and broke off in the full flight of his eloquence, as he saw something like a hand come and take down the top brick from the face of paint which he had laid over the little door in the palace-wall which Wio-Wani had so beautifully painted. In another moment there was no doubt about it; brick by brick the wall was being pulled down, in spite of its double thickness.

The lecturer was altogether too dumbfounded and terrified to utter a word. He and all his apprentices stood round and stared while the demolition of the wall proceeded. Before long he recognised Wio-Wani with his flowing white beard; it was his handiwork this pulling down of the wall! He still had a brick in his hand when he stepped through the opening that he had made, and close after him stepped Tiki-Pu!

Tiki-Pu had grown tall and strong—he was even handsome; but for all that his old master recognised him, and saw with an envious foreboding that under his arms he carried many rolls and stretchers and portfolios, and other belongings of his craft. Clearly Tiki-Pu was coming back into the world, and was going to be a great painter.

Down the garden path came Wio-Wani, and Tiki-Pu walked after him; Tiki-Pu was so tall that his head stood well over Wio-Wani's shoulders—old man and young man together made a handsome pair.

How big Wio-Wani grew as he walked down the avenues of his garden and into the foreground of his picture! and how big the brick in his hand! and ah, how angry he seemed!

Wio-Wani came right down to the edge of the picture-frame and held up the brick. 'What did you do that for?' he asked.

'I . . . didn't!' Tiki-Pu's old master was beginning to

reply; and the lie was still rolling on his tongue when the weight of the brick-bat, hurled by the stout arm of Wio-Wani, felled him. After that he never spoke again. That brick-bat, which he himself had reared, became his own tombstone.

Just inside the picture-frame stood Tiki-Pu, kissing the wonderful hands of Wio-Wani, which had taught him all their skill. 'Good-bye, Tiki-Pu!' said Wio-Wani, embracing him tenderly. 'Now I am sending my second self into the world. When you are tired and want rest, come back to me: old Wio-Wani will take you in.'

Tiki-Pu was sobbing and the tears were running down his cheeks as he stepped out of Wio-Wani's wonderfully painted garden and stood once more upon earth. Turning, he saw the old man walking away along the path towards the little door under the palace-wall. At the door Wio-Wani turned and waved his hand for the last time. Tiki-Pu still stood watching him. Then the door opened and shut, and Wio-Wani was gone. Softly as a flower the picture seemed to have folded its leaves over him.

Tiki-Pu leaned a wet face against the picture and kissed the door in the palace-wall which Wio-Wani had painted so beautifully. 'O Wio-Wani, dear master,' he cried, 'are you there?'

He waited, and called again, but no voice answered him.

From *Moonshine and Clover* by Laurence Housman (Jonathan Cape, London)

(See Note, page 210)

The Young Man with Music in his Fingers

Once upon a time there was a young man who went out into the world to seek his fortune with nothing but a pleasant face, good health, and a kind heart.

He had not gone far before he came to a forest and heard such a clamour of birds, as if all the birds of the air were gathered together in that one place and making a noise.

When he went into the forest to see what was afoot he found a Jenny Wren caught fast in a snare, and all her friends and relations, and even her casual acquaintances sitting round her on the branches of trees and bushes, weeping and wailing and scolding and screeching, which may have consoled her, but was of little practical value.

The youth, however, took pity on her and at once set her free. And now there was such a sweet sound of rejoicing and whistling and cooing, you would have thought that all the Springs for a hundred years were being celebrated all at once.

And Jenny Wren flew up on the young man's shoulder, and thanking him prettily for his timely aid, told him that she in return would give him a gift.

'Only blow upon your fingers,' she said, 'and you shall make such music as if all the flutes in the world were being played by skilled musicians.'

So the youth put up his fingers and blew upon them, and sure enough, it was just as Jenny Wren had said. There was the sweet sound of flutes in that forest as if all the musicians in the world were blowing on their flutes at a king's banquet.

So the youth thanked Jenny Wren and was glad to see how gaily now she flew away, and on he went well pleased at his accomplishment.

He went on with his travels until at last he came to the sea, and was walking on the shore wondering how he should go further when he suddenly noticed a flashing of silver among the dark rocks and he heard the sound of splashing water, and hurrying over to where it was he saw a fine fish which had been left high and dry in a small rock pool, and the tide had gone back and left it.

He saw how desperately it was flapping about under the hot noon sun and he was sorry for it, so he caught it in his hands and carried it from the shallow pool and threw it once more into the deep water of the sea, and was glad to see the splendid shining of its scales as it plunged proudly down into the deep water.

But before it disappeared it swam close to the rock on which he was standing.

'Twang upon your fingers,' said the fish, 'and you shall make the music of harps, as if all the waters of the world were running sweetly down to the sea.'

So the youth twanged upon his fingers and it was just as the fish had said, and there was the noise of harps playing as if all the harps in the world were being plucked by skilled musicians.

So he thanked the fish and went on his way well pleased with this new accomplishment.

Well, he found a boat by the sea and he crossed over it in the boat and came to a strange land.

He went ashore and found a savage wilderness, and he began to journey through it, and dreary and desolate he found it.

Now as he was going forward he suddenly heard a great roaring, and the tall grass through which he went trembled and bent low before the sound.

So terrible was the roaring that at first he was afraid; but he was a bold youth and did not like to go back, so on he went and came to a pit cunningly dug in the ground, and a

young lion had fallen into it, and its mother and father and
three young brothers were standing round, looking into the
pit and bewailing its fate with their terrible cries.

Now, he might well have been more frightened than before,
but his pity for the poor beasts quite overcame his fear, and
climbing down into the pit he lifted up the young lion in his
arms and put it once more at its mother's side. Then climbing
out again he rejoiced to see how gaily it ran about and how
proudly the parents tossed their great heads with joy.

He was about to continue on his way when the lion approached him and said :

'For restoring our son to safety I will give you a gift. Only
clap your hands together and the noise will be as if all the
drummers of all the armies in the world were beating on
their drums.'

So the youth did as the lion said and clapped his hands,
and at once, such a tattooing and drumming and rub-a-dub
dubbing, as if a thousand thousand drummer boys were let
loose with their drums to make as much noise as they could
for the king's coronation.

So here was the youth with yet another talent, and on he
went well pleased with himself as well he might be.

Then he passed out of the wilderness and came among men,
and went through villages and cultivated land, and saw a
town in the distance where the king of that country lived.
He was hurrying to reach it before nightfall when he heard
a wailing coming from a field at the side of the road, and he
found lying under the bushes a tiny child quite exhausted and
scarcely breathing.

So he picked it up and carried it into the next village,
which he found in a state of great confusion, for the child
had strayed from its mother's side in the harvest field and
for three days and nights had been lost, and everyone had
joined in the search, but with no result, and they had all
despaired of ever seeing it again.

Well, as you can imagine, they were all rejoiced to see him approaching, the child in his arms, and its parents made him stay by them for the night, and nothing they could do was too much for them. And in the morning, as he was about to set forth, the mother said:

'I will give you a gift for bringing me back my child. If ever you open your mouth to sing the sound shall be like a choir of sweet singers singing at a festival in honour of the king.'

And the young man opened his mouth and sang, and the sound was even as she had said. So he thanked her for her gift and went rejoicing on his way towards the city.

Now as he drew near the city gates he noticed all the people going in, and he saw a tiny hovel just beside the gates, and an old woman sitting there, her cat by her side. And as the people went by her she greeted each one, and asked them where they were going and where they had come from, and how they fared and what was their business.

But such a miserable old thing she seemed that most of those who passed took no notice of her, a few cursed her, many told her rudely they were about their own business, and not one of them gave her a civil answer or returned her greeting.

But when the young man came by and she hailed him, he returned her a good morrow, and told her where he came from, and how he was seeking his fortune, and as for how he fared, he fared well and wished the same to her. And he stooped and tickled the cat under its chin, and it shut its eyes and purred.

'You are a polite young man,' said the old woman, 'and that is a rare thing hereabouts. As for me, I am a Wise Woman, and if you will lodge in my house I can help you to come by the fortune you seek.'

So he thanked her and went in, and then she told him that so many people were coming into the city because the king's only daughter had come of an age to marry, and at noon this day heralds at the gate of the palace would declare the conditions of her choice.

So at noon that day the young man went with many others and stood at the gates of the palace. And as the hour struck the Princess herself appeared on a golden throne set up in the courtyard of the palace, and at her side were heralds in scarlet and gold who blew loud blasts on their trumpets and cried in a loud voice:

'Listen to me, all you people, and then you shall hear of that which must be done.

'The Princess will marry no-one until she is properly crowned. And the crown with which she wishes to be crowned is thus.

'It shall be fashioned of the lightning snapped from the fingers of the Mad Man of the Sky.

'It shall be set with the seven rubies which shine among the scales of the Old Serpent of the Earth and the seven green emeralds that hang in the hair of the Ancient Maiden of the Sea.

'If this you cannot bring to her, then she will have none of you, but shall live and die a maiden, and the country at her death will be left without a ruler, and woe betide the people if that day should come!'

And again they blew on their trumpets, and the people began to murmur, and soon there was a great noise of talk, some rejoicing that all men were free to try to win the maiden. 'For,' said these, 'one man is as good as another, and you or I are as likely to win the treasures with which to fashion her crown as anyone else.'

But though they spoke so hopefully, they didn't seem very clear as to how they should set about it.

And the rest of the people, and most of the old ones among them, bewailed these hard conditions, and were full of fore-boding.

'Be sure,' these said, 'the land will be left without a ruler, and then you may be certain there will be trouble and wars, and no peace anywhere, and injustice and evil, and all were better dead.'

But the young man when he heard what the heralds had said was well enough pleased. No sooner had he seen the Princess where she sat on her throne than he had no thought beside than to marry her.

'And if the conditions are hard,' he thought, 'my rivals will be all the fewer.'

So he went back quickly to the Wise Woman and told her all about it, and asked her how he might find the Old Serpent of the Earth, for he thought he would come to him more easily than to either of the others. 'And I may as well start by succeeding, even if in the end I fail.'

So the Wise Woman told him how he should find the lair of the Old Serpent, in the side of a dark mountain at the furthest ends of the earth.

'But beware,' she said, 'how you approach him. For he is old and terrible, and has moreover not slept these thousand thousand years. And this, as you can imagine, has not improved his temper. And if you approach him, you do so at your own risk, for I would not go near him. No! Not for all the rubies in the world.'

'Oh! well,' said the youth, 'but you are not wooing a maiden, and that makes all the difference, as everyone knows.'

And he thanked her for her directions, and away he went just as she had told him.

He travelled without ceasing for seven days and seven nights, and then he came to the dark mountain at the furthest ends of the earth, and here it was the Old Serpent had his lair.

So he boldly went up the face of the mountain till he came to the entrance of a dark cavern, and very dark and dismal it looked, and he feared going into that place, knowing what he would find there.

But then he bethought himself of his accomplishments.

'I have heard,' he thought, 'that serpents have a liking for sweet sounds. I will play to him the sweet music of flutes, and if that fails to please him I am a lost man.'

So he sat down at the grisly entrance of the cave and he blew on his fingers, and he blew and he blew, and such sweet music was made as if all the flutes in the world were blown upon softly by skilled musicians, and the extreme sweetness of the noise sounded strange in that grim place.

Then as he played he felt the earth begin to shake beneath him.

'Ah! here is the old one bestirring himself,' he said, and grew pale, as well he might.

But he went on blowing on his fingers, and soon, from the dark recesses of the cavern, he saw the great serpent up-rearing, its golden scales set with precious stones glowing dimly in the dark, and he saw its shining eyes, cold and bright as diamonds and his hands and feet grew clammy and cold, and his mouth dry as he met its hard unwinking stare.

But still he blew upon his fingers and made soft music, and at last the huge serpent began to swing and sway. And as it uncoiled itself and reared itself up in that vast cavern the whole mountain shook, and the whole world with it, for it had not so bestirred itself for a million years and more.

'Who are you?' it said at last. 'It is well for you that you make sweet music, for had you disturbed me otherwise, you would not have long regretted it.'

'I am come,' said the youth, 'to ask you a favour. Give me the seven red rubies set in the scales of your head. For the maiden I want to marry must have them in her crown, or else she will not marry, but will live and die a maid.'

'You are brave,' said the serpent, 'to come asking favours of me. But only go on playing the music you were making for seven days and seven nights without ceasing and then I will sleep. And that I have not done for a thousand thousand years, and for that I will gladly give you the jewels you are seeking.'

So the youth set himself down and for seven days and seven nights he blew on his fingers without ceasing, and all that time the rocky wilderness echoed and re-echoed to the sweet sound of flutes, and the Old Serpent coiled itself up, and its hard, unwinking eyes were closed, and such a deep peace fell on the place and on the whole earth people marvelled and wondered what it could mean.

At the end of that time the youth stopped playing, and on the instant the Old Serpent was awake.

'I have not heard such music since the stars took up their station in the sky,' it said. And it sighed, and it was as if the earth shook itself and was awake.

Then the serpent let the youth approach, and he took the seven red rubies from the other bright jewels set in the scales of its head, and wrapping them up in his kerchief and tying it to his belt the young man thanked the serpent and turned his back on that lonely place, and though he came out unharmed he was not sorry to be gone.

Then he made his way back to the city, and the Wise Woman at the gate, and he told her all that had happened and gave her the jewels to look after while he went seeking the others, and asked her how he should come to the Ancient Maiden of the Sea, to get the seven green emeralds the princess wanted for her crown.

So the Wise Woman told him how he must go to the edge of the sea, and unless he could win her to come up to him he would never hold speech with her, for she sat in her palace ten thousand fathoms deep in the middle of the sea, and so hated the light and the sounds and sight of men that she had not come to the surface for a hundred thousand years.

'And if,' said the Wise Woman, 'you manage to rouse her now, even so, I would not change places with you. For she has only to stir a finger and all the waters of the world will rise up and engulf you. And I would not risk that for all the jewels in her hair!'

'Oh! well,' said the youth, 'but you are not wooing a maiden. And that, as I said before, makes all the difference.'

So he listened carefully to her directions and thanked her for her help, and away he went, his spirits high.

For seven days and seven nights he travelled without ceasing and then he came to the shore of the deepest ocean and he saw how it spread out before him to the far edge of the sky.

Remembering how the Ancient Maiden of the Sea hated the light, he sat down on a rock to await the coming of darkness, and blessed his luck that it was a moonless night.

At the very darkest hour of midnight, by the pale light of the stars, he made his way out on to a rock which jutted far into the sea, and there he sat down on the glistening seaweed and began to twang upon his fingers and to make the sweet noise of harps playing as if all the harps in the world were being plucked by skilled musicians.

It was not long before he saw the water begin to shake, and he felt afraid, as well he might all alone by the edge of the sea and only the Ancient Maiden coming to keep him company.

But he did not falter, but kept twanging on his fingers, and in the dim starlight he saw the surface of the sea begin to heave and break, and the cold light of phosphorus flickering in the depths, and then out of the sea rose up the Ancient Maiden, her skin pale and white and glistening with drops of water, and her face beautiful and terrible, the face of a young maiden but old with the wisdom of ages, and her eyes were dark and unfathomable with no light in their darkness, and her long green hair floated all around her like trailing seaweed on the surface of the water.

'Who are you?' she said. 'For a hundred thousand years no-one has disturbed me. And I so hate man and his works and ways that I set myself down in the deepest part of the sea to avoid him. And now, you, with the sweet music you make, as if all the waters of the world were flowing sweetly down to the sea, have drawn me up from my silence and darkness to the light of the stars and the sound of your music.'

So then he told her why he had come and what he was seeking, and indeed he could see the faint glimmer of the gems set in the darkness of her hair.

'Play to me again,' she said, 'but speak no more, for your voice is as the voice of all men, harsh to my ears. But for the sake of your music I will give you what you ask.'

So he sat there on the wet rock and twanged on his fingers and made her music all through the night until the stars grew pale and the sky grew light at the edge of the sea, and the Sea Maiden shuddered and cried to him to be still.

'Play no more,' she said, 'for the sweetness of the sounds holds me, but I fear the light and dare not stay.'

And she plucked the seven green stones from her hair and threw them up on to the rock, and plunged swiftly down into the deep salt water, and he saw the flash of her white body and the floating strands of her hair and the foam white where she had plunged away, and then she was gone.

So he took the seven green emeralds where they lay on the rock and wrapped them in his kerchief and tied them to his belt and turned his back on the sea and made his way as soon as he could back to the city and the Wise Woman at the gate.

He told her all that had happened and gave her the seven green emeralds to put with the seven red rubies until he should bring the gold in which they must be set. And he asked her how he should find the Mad Man of the Sky, in the snapping of whose fingers was the lightning which must furnish the gold for the maiden's crown.

The Wise Woman told him how he should find him, but warned him that if he did so he would certainly regret it.

'For the Mad Man of the Sky has sudden fits of violence, and when these fits are on him the sky is filled with hurricanes and tempests, and thunderbolts hurtle through the air and woe betide anyone who should be near him at such a time. And besides these fits of violence the Mad Man of the Sky is proud. So proud that he despises man and his puny ways and sits high up among the clouds and laughs at our antics, and blows with his breath to torment us with fierce winds, and spits upon us so that the rivers and seas are flooded and overflow their limits, and he claps his hands together so that thunder and lightning shall strike terror into the small hearts of men. And as for me,' she concluded, 'I would not go to that one. No! Not for all the gold in creation.'

'Oh! well,' said the youth, 'But you know, I go to win a maiden, and there's the difference, as I have said before.'

So he said good-bye to the Wise Woman and thanked her for her directions, and away he went travelling for seven days and seven nights without ceasing.

At the end of that time he came to the edge of the sky and stood there, the immense distances of air before him.

Well, certainly it seemed improbable that his voice, however loud he shouted, should reach to the furthest limit of that expanse of space and bring the Mad Man of the Sky to have speech with him.

So then he bethought himself of his third talent, and he began to clap his hands together. And then, such a noise of beating drums the sky shook with the volume of the sound, and the very furthest corners of space were filled with the drumming, and the sky echoed and re-echoed to the music he made.

He had not been clapping long when he saw huge clouds come rolling together, and in the midst of them the vast shape of him he was seeking, and he felt himself small and afraid before him as well he might.

But he went on clapping and the drumming never ceased, and at last the Mad Man of the Sky saw him and said:

'For twice ten thousand years I have sat in my cloudy fastness and have held myself aloof from the small affairs of men, and have despised them and their works and have held no truck with them. But who are you to make music I myself might be glad to make, and why do you come and brave the thunderbolts I hold in the palm of my hand, and the sharp lightning I can flash from the snapping of my fingers?'

'It is that very lightning I have come for,' said the youth, 'for without I make her a crown of it I shall never win the maiden on whom my heart is set.'

'Well,' said the Mad Man of the Sky. 'You are a bold youth, and I like such a one. But you cannot have my golden lightning merely for the asking. But if you can earn it honestly, you shall have as much as you wish for.

'When I let out my winds from the cave in which they are kept, I do so, telling them to return to me as soon as they hear the rolling of my thunder, so.' And the Mad Man of the Sky clapped his hands, clap, clap, clap, clap, first fast and then slow, and at once there was a rolling of thunder all round the sky and a sudden rushing of winds past the youth where he was standing, his clothes were well nigh torn from his back and he himself bowled over.

'You see,' said the Mad Man, laughing, 'they are afraid to disobey me.' And he clapped his hands together again with a great bang just to hurry up the loiterers.

'But this is how it is,' he went on, and his face grew dark and gloomy and his hands trembled.

'A hundred thousand years ago a little wind went out to-gether with some others, a little wind, the fairest of all the winds who haunt the caverns of space. It went out with the others, but it did not return. I made my thunder go rumbling round the sky, till heaven and earth were so filled with the sound that people thought it was the end of Time and fell on their knees with terror and began to pray.

'But still that little wind did not return, and when I questioned the others, they said this wind on going out had laughed and said, "If I do not hear the summons to return I cannot be said to have disobeyed the summons. I will go so far that not even our master's loudest thundering can reach me, and then I shall be free to dance and whistle and sing for ever and ever." And away it had fled so swiftly that by the time I thundered to bring them all home again it had gone so far into space that thunder as I might it did not hear me, and I have not seen it since.

'Now, if you with your drumming can reach the ears of that wind and bring it home, then my lightning shall be yours and my thanks into the bargain.'

Well, that was an admission to win from so proud and surly an old creature!

So then the youth began to clap his hands, first gently and slowly, CLAP CLAP CLAP, and there was the noise of rolling drums that set the air vibrating.

Then louder he clapped and faster, and the rolling of the drums grew and grew, BANG BANG BANG—RUB DUB A DUB DUB, the whole of space and beyond was filled with the sound of the drumming, DUM DURRA DRUMM DRUMM—BOOM BEROOM BOOM, till even the Mad Man of the Sky began to roll his eyes and twitch his fingers.

And the young man clapped and clapped, and suddenly his hair was stirred by a soft warm wind, and the sweet cool air blew on his cheek, and the Mad Man of the Sky burst out laughing and clapped his hands, and then what a noise there was with the two of them at it together!

So then the young man stopped his clapping, and the Mad Man of the Sky held out his hands as if he were holding something.

'See,' he cried, 'my little wind has come home again. Ah! you little villain, you thought you could cheat even me!' And he laughed again with delight and stroked it and spoke to it fondly, like a father, though the young man could see nothing there.

'Well, now indeed you shall have what you ask for,' said the Mad Man of the Sky. And with that he snapped his fingers, and a sharp flash of forked lightning came suddenly forth, so bright the young man was blinded, but he snatched at the brightness as it went by and caught it fast and thrust it quickly into his kerchief, which he tied at his belt. Then he thanked the Mad Man of the Sky and turned back to the earth and the dwellings of men, and now he went gaily, for his task was nearly accomplished.

When he got back to the city he went to the Wise Woman at the gate.

'See,' he said, 'now I have the gold and the emeralds and

the rubies. All that remains to be done is to fashion the crown, and that will soon be done.'

So he took the gold from his kerchief to work it into shape. But here was a pretty pass! He no sooner shook it free from the kerchief than his eyes were so dazzled by the light that he could see nothing, and as for doing fine work on it he might as well throw it on the dung heap for all the good he could make of it!

While he was standing in dismay not knowing what to do, his eyes turned away from it, the Wise Woman came up to him.

'Do not despair,' she said, 'but wrap it up again in your kerchief and take it to the blind smith who lives alone in the wilderness. If you can please him, he will do it, and no man better, although his eyes are blind. For your gold is so bright that no other man could do it save only he who has no sight in his eyes to be dazzled by it.'

So the young man wrapped up the gold again and took the emeralds and rubies, and he found out the place where the blind smith was working, in a lonely place far away in a wilderness, for he was a sorrowful man and shunned company.

When he came there he found the blind smith sitting outside the cave in which he lived and worked.

'I have found you at last,' cried the youth, 'and right glad am I to have done so. For if you can fashion me a crown set with these emeralds and rubies I shall win such a maiden to wife as no man had before or since.'

'I can do anything if I will, but I won't,' said the smith, sitting still and scowling. 'What do I care if you win you a maiden or no? I have lost the sight of my eyes and the world is a dark place to me, and why should I make it fair for another?'

'Have you no pleasures left?' said the youth.

'Aye,' said the smith. 'Now that I am blind I take pleasure

through my ears, and the sound of sweet singing can make me forget my sorrows. But the birds are afraid to come near me, frightened by the noise I make at my work, and as for men, if there be sweet singers among them they take good care to keep their own distance.'

'I will sing you a song,' said the youth, and he opened his mouth to sing, and at once the wilderness was filled with the sound of a choir of sweet singers singing in honour of the king.

When he had done, the blind smith got up and held out his hand for the gold and never said a word.

But the young man gave it to him and the emeralds and rubies also, and he turned away from the brightness which suddenly shone out into the cave and only listened to the roaring of the fire when the smith used the bellows, and the tap tap tapping as he worked at the metal.

All night long the smith was working, and in the morning he cried to the young man.

'You sang sweetly, and I carry the sound still in my ears. Take the crown I have fashioned and good luck to you and your maiden.'

And the young man came and took the crown, and though the brightness made him blink he could see that it was beautiful.

So he thanked the smith, and again sang him a song, and away he went, whistling and singing to himself he was so light of heart.

When he came again to the Wise Woman she tidied him up and gave him her blessing, and hiding the crown in his kerchief he boldly went to the gates of the palace.

'I am come to claim the king's daughter,' he said, 'and I have the crown here in my kerchief.'

The gatekeeper looked at him sourly.

'As like as not,' he said, 'they all say the same thing. There are already ninety and nine of you young men and

each one with the crown in his kerchief and each will win
the maiden, they have no doubt of that! Well, come along in,
and to-night you shall spend in feasting, and to-morrow you
shall present yourselves. For the princess has said that when
a hundred of you are come there shall be a showing of
crowns, and if none of you have the right one, bad luck to
all of you.'

So the youth went in, and that night was feasted and en-
tertained with the ninety and nine other young men, and
they looked at him disdainfully in his poor clothes, for they
were all rich and fine, and had a need to be, seeing that to
produce a crown they had been about buying the finest gold
and rubies and emeralds they could lay their hands on,
hoping that the maiden would not notice that these were not
the jewels and gold she had asked for.

Well, the very next day the suitors were led into the great
hall of the palace and the Princess sat high upon her throne,
and her mother and father at her side, and you may be sure
there was no-one in the world more beautiful.

Then one by one the young men came forward and put
their crowns on the steps of her throne, and such a shining
of golden crowns, each one worked more gorgeously than the
last, and you would have thought that nothing could have
been more magnificent.

But when the ninety-ninth crown was set at her feet the
maiden's face was sad, for well she knew the crown she had
asked for was not among these.

Then forward came the youth and undid his kerchief, and
all in the great court of the palace hid their eyes, for the
shining of that crown had the sharpness of lightning, and
the red of those rubies was like the heart of the fire, and the
green of those emeralds like the cold green light of icebergs
floating on the waters of polar seas.

And when the maiden saw it she smiled at the youth, and
bade him come up and put the crown on her head. And this

was strange. For of all that company he and she were the only two who could look on the crown and not be blinded by its splendour, and now that he could look upon it he saw that the blind smith had worked well, and no crown before or since was so finely made as this.

So then they were married and the young man took his place on the throne beside the Princess, and all the people of the land rejoiced, for now they need not fear one day to be without a ruler.

And the young man caused a little house to be built in the fairest part of the palace grounds, and this he gave to the Wise Woman, that she should live there in comfort with her cat till the end of her days. And the maiden, after her wedding, gave her bright crown to the Wise Woman that she should hide it away in some secret place, for it was too rare and too bright to be seen at all times by all men.

And as for the celebration of the wedding, nothing could be finer! For the young man himself made all the music, blowing and twanging on his fingers, clapping his hands together and singing, so it seemed that all the flutes and harps and drums in the world were playing together in concert, and choirs of sweet singers were singing in chorus, till the oldest feet were dancing and the saddest hearts laughing.

From *The Wild Cherry* by Diana Ross (Faber and Faber, London)

(See Note, page 211)

The Jolly Tailor who Became King

Once upon a time, in the town of Taidaraida, there lived a merry little Tailor, Mr Joseph Nitechka. He was a very thin man and had a beard of one hundred and thirty-six hairs.

All tailors are thin, reminding one of a needle and thread, but Mr Nitechka was the thinnest of all, for he could pass through the eye of his own needle. But for all this he was a very happy man, and a handsome one too, particularly when on holidays he braided his beard.

Now Mr Nitechka would have lived very happily in Taidaraida had it not been for a Gypsy. She happened to be in the town when she cut her foot. In her trouble she went to the Tailor, who darned the skin so carefully and neatly that not a scar could be seen. The Gypsy was so grateful that she read Nitechka's fortune from his hand:

'If you leave this town on a Sunday and walk always westwards, you will reach a place where you will be chosen King.'

Nitechka laughed at this. But that very night he dreamt that he indeed became a King, and from great prosperity he grew so fat that he looked like an immense barrel. Upon waking, he thought:

'Maybe it is true? Who knows? Get up, Mr Nitechka, and go West.'

He took a bundle with a hundred needles and a thousand miles of thread, a thimble, an iron, and a pair of very big scissors, and started out to find the West. But no one knew where it was. Finally he asked an old man, a hundred and six years old, who, after thinking a while, said:

'West must be where the sun sets.'

63

This seemed so wise to Nitechka that he went that way. But he had not gone far when a gust of wind blew across the field—not a very strong gust—but, because Mr Nitechka was so exceedingly thin, just enough to carry him off.

The Tailor flew through the air, laughing heartily at such a ride. Soon, however, the Wind became tired and let him

down to earth. He was much bewildered and did not come to his senses until someone shouted:

'What is this?'

Mr Nitechka looked around and saw that he was in a big wheat field and the wind had thrown him right into the arms of a Scarecrow. The Scarecrow was very elegant in a green jacket and a broken stove-pipe hat, and his trousers were only a little bit torn. He had two sticks for feet and also sticks for hands.

Mr Nitechka took off his little cap, and bowed very low, saying in his thin voice:

'My regards to the honourable Sir. I beg your pardon if I stepped on your foot. I am Mr Nitechka, the Tailor.'

'I am very pleased to meet such a charming man,' answered the Scarecrow. 'I am Count Scarecrow and my coat of arms is Four Sticks. I watch the sparrows here so that they will not steal wheat, but I give little heed to them. I am uncommonly courageous and would like to fight only with lions and tigers, but this year they very seldom come to eat the wheat. Where are you going, Mr Nitechka?'

Nitechka bowed again and hopped three times as he was very polite and he knew that well bred men greeted each other thus.

'Where do I go, Mr Count? I am going Westward to a place where I shall be chosen King.'

'Is it possible?'

'Of course! I was born to be a King. And perhaps you, Mr Count, would like to go with me; it will be merrier.'

'All right,' answered the Scarecrow. 'I am already weary of being here. But please, Mr Nitechka, mend my clothes a bit, because I might like to marry someone on the way; and so I should be neat and handsome.'

'With great pleasure!' said Nitechka. He went to work and in an hour the Scarecrow had a beautiful suit and a hat almost like new. The sparrows in the field laughed at him a little, but he paid no attention to them as he walked with great dignity with Mr Nitechka.

On the way the two became great friends. They generally slept in a wheat field, the Tailor tying himself to the Scarecrow with a piece of thread so that the wind could not carry him off again. And when dogs attacked them, the Scarecrow, who was very brave because of his profession, tore off his foot and threw it after them. Then he tied it again to his body.

Once in the evening they spied a light through the trees.

'Let us go there; maybe they will let us pass the night,' said Nitechka.

'By all means, let us do them that honour,' answered the Scarecrow.

As they drew nearer they saw that it was a strange house because it could walk. It stood on four feet and was turning round.

'The owner of the house must be a gay man,' whispered the Tailor. 'He dances all the time.'

They waited until the door came round to them and then went into the house. It was indeed a very strange house. Although it was summer, immense logs of wood burned in the stove, and on the fire sat a nobleman warming himself. From time to time he took a glowing coal in his hands and swallowed it with great pleasure. Upon noticing the travellers, he went over to them and bowed and said:

'Is it not Mr Nitechka and Count Scarecrow?'

They were speechless with astonishment to think that he should know them, but said nothing. Mr Nitechka hopped three times and Count Scarecrow took off his hat.

The nobleman continued:

'Stay with me for supper and tomorrow you may go your way. I will call my wife, my daughter, and my other relatives.'

He clapped his hands and suddenly a large company appeared. The host's daughter was very beautiful, but when she laughed, it was as if a horse neighed in the meadow. She took an instant liking to Nitechka and told him that she would very much like to have him for her husband. They sat down to supper, Nitechka and Count Scarecrow on a bench, and all the others on iron pots filled with glowing coals.

'Do not wonder, dear Sirs,' the host said, 'that we sit thus, for our family always feels very cold.'

They served soup in a big cauldron and Nitechka was just

putting his spoon to his lips, when Count Scarecrow pulled his coat and whispered:

'Mr Nitechka, don't eat, for this is hot pitch!'

So pretending that they liked the soup, they spilt it under the table. Then a strange looking servant brought a dish of filleted devil-fish, and one of rats in a black sauce, and later he served fried locust, glow-worms with phosphorus, and for dessert prickly pears and dead sea apples. Nitechka and Count Scarecrow threw everything under the table, becoming more and more frightened.

All at once the host said:

'Do you know, Mr Nitechka, that the King has just died in Patsanoff?'

'Where is Patsanoff, is it far?' asked the Tailor.

'A crow can fly to that town in two days. And do you know that they are seeking a King there, and he who marries my daughter shall be King?'

The girl neighed like an old horse at this and threw her arms around Nitechka's neck.

'Let's run away!' murmured Count Scarecrow.

'But I can't find the door!' replied Mr Nitechka.

Soon, however, the whole family became very gay, and presently the host said:

'We will drink to your health and sing merrily. Do you know a song, Mr Nitechka?'

'Yes, indeed,' said Nitechka, 'and a very nice one.'

Saying this, he whispered to Count Scarecrow:

'Watch, brother, and when the door is behind us, shout!'

Then he got up, took off his little cap, and in his thin little voice began to sing the only song he knew:—

> 'Sing praises to the Holy Virgin,
>   Sing praises to Her Wondrous Name.'

At the mention of the Virgin, the whole family rose to their feet, and ran around the room, sprawling and shouting and cursing. Nitechka said nothing, but simply continued his song. He could feel the house running somewhere with them, and so he sang and sang like the thinnest pipe in the organ. When he had finished the song, he began to sing it all over again. At that moment everything disappeared, and only a terrible wind blew.

Terrified, Nitechka and Count Scarecrow found themselves alone in a huge meadow. Then they gave thanks for their delivery and Nitechka said:

'They were awful devils, but we overpowered them.'

'I frightened them so much,' boasted Count Scarecrow.

They continued their way towards Patsanoff, a beautiful old town where the King had died. When after seven days of adventures they reached Patsanoff, they were greatly astonished. All around the town it was sunshiny and pleasant; but over Patsanoff the rain poured from the sky as from a bucket.

'I won't go in there,' said the Scarecrow, 'because my hat will get wet.'

'And even I do not wish to become King of such a wet kingdom,' said the Tailor.

Just then the townspeople spied them and rushed towards them, led by the Burgomaster riding on a goat.

'Dear Sirs,' they said, 'maybe you can help us.'

'And what has happened to you?' asked Nitechka.

'Deluge and destruction threaten us. Our King died a week ago, and since that time a terrible rain has come upon our gorgeous town. We cannot even make fires in our houses, because so much water runs through the chimneys. We will perish, honourable Sirs!'

'It is too bad,' said Nitechka very wisely.

'Oh, very bad! And we are most sorry for the late King's daughter as the poor thing can't stop crying and this causes even more water.'

'That makes it still worse,' replied Nitechka still more wisely.

'Help us, help us!' continued the Burgomaster. 'Do you know the immeasurable reward the Princess promises to the one who stops the rain? She promises to marry him and then he will become King.'

'Truly?' cried Nitechka. 'Count Scarecrow, let us go to the town. We ought to try and help them.'

They were led through the terrible rain to the Princess, who upon seeing Nitechka, cried out:

'Oh, what a handsome youth!'

He hopped three times and said:

'Is it true, Princess, that you will marry the one who stops the rain?'

'I vowed I would.'

'And if *I* do?'

'I shall keep my promise.'

'And I shall become King?'

'You will, oh beautiful youth.'

'Very well,' answered the Tailor, 'I am going to stop the rain.'

So saying he nodded to Count Scarecrow and they left the Princess.

The whole population, full of hope, gathered round them. Nitechka and Count Scarecrow stood under an umbrella and whispered to each other:

'Listen, Scarecrow, what shall we do to make the rain stop falling?'

'We have to bring back pleasant weather.'

'But how?'

'Ha! Let's think.'

But for three days they thought and the rain fell and fell and fell. Suddenly Nitechka gave a cry of joy like a goat's bleating.

'I know where the rain comes from!'

'Where from?'

'From the sky!'

'Eh!' grumbled the Scarecrow. 'I know that too. Surely it doesn't fall from the bottom to the top, but the other way round.'

'Yes,' said Nitechka, 'but why does it fall over the town only and not elsewhere?'

'Because elsewhere is nice weather.'

'You're stupid, Mr Count,' said the Tailor. 'But tell me how long has it rained?'

'They say since the King died.'

'So you see! Now I know everything! The King was so great and mighty that when he died and went to Heaven he made a huge hole in the sky.'

'Oh, oh, true!'

'Through the hole the rain poured and it will pour until the end of the world if the hole isn't sewed up!'

Count Scarecrow looked at him in amazement.

'In all my life I have never seen such a wise Tailor,' said he.

They rejoiced greatly, went to the Burgomaster, and ordered him to tell the townspeople that Mr Joseph Nitechka, a citizen of the town of Taidaraida, promised to stop the rain.

'Long live Mr Nitechka! Long may he live!' shouted the whole town.

Then Nitechka ordered them to bring all the ladders in the town, tie them together, and lean them against the sky. He took a hundred needles and, threading one, went up the ladders. Count Scarecrow stayed at the bottom and un-wound the spool on which there was a thousand miles of thread.

When Nitechka got to the very top he saw that there was a huge hole in the sky, a hole as big as the town. A torn piece of the sky hung down, and through the hole the water poured.

So he went to work and sewed and sewed for two days. His fingers grew stiff and he became very tired but he did not stop. When he had finished sewing he pressed out the sky with the iron and then, exhausted, went down the ladders.

Once more the sun shone over Patsanoff, Count Scarecrow went almost mad with joy, as did all the inhabitants of the town. The Princess wiped her eyes, and throwing herself on Nitechka's neck, kissed him affectionately.

Nitechka was very happy. He looked around, and there were the Burgomaster and Councilmen bringing him a golden sceptre and a gorgeous crown and shouting:

'Long live King Nitechka! Long live he! Long live he! And let him be the Princess' husband and reign happily!'

So the merry little Tailor reigned happily for a long time, and the rain never fell in his kingdom. In his good fortune Nitechka did not forget his old friend, Count Scarecrow, but appointed him the Great Warden of the Kingdom to drive away the sparrows from the Royal head.

From *The Jolly Tailor and Other Fairy Tales* translated from the Polish by Lucia M. Borski and Kate B. Miller (David McKay, N.Y.)

(See Note, page 212)

The Selfish Giant

Every afternoon, as they were coming from school, the children used to go and play in the Giant's garden.

It was a large lovely garden, with soft green grass. Here and there over the grass stood beautiful flowers like stars, and there were twelve peach-trees that in the spring-time broke out into delicate blossoms of pink and pearl, and in the autumn bore rich fruit. The birds sat on the trees and sang so sweetly that the children used to stop their games in order to listen to them. 'How happy we are here!' they cried to each other.

One day the Giant came back. He had been to visit his friend the Cornish ogre, and had stayed with him for seven years. After the seven years were over he had said all that he had to say, for his conversation was limited, and he determined to return to his own castle. When he arrived he saw the children playing in the garden.

'What are you doing here?' he cried in a very gruff voice, and the children ran away.

'My own garden is my own garden,' said the Giant; 'anyone can understand that, and I will allow nobody to play in it but myself.'

So he built a high wall all round it, and put up a notice-board.

TRESPASSERS
WILL BE
PROSECUTED

He was a very selfish Giant.

The poor children had now nowhere to play. They tried

to play on the road, but the road was very dusty and full of hard stones, and they did not like it. They used to wander round the high walls when their lessons were over, and talk about the beautiful garden inside.

'How happy we were there!' they said to each other.

Then the Spring came, and all over the country there were little blossoms and little birds. Only in the garden of the Selfish Giant it was still winter. The birds did not care to sing in it as there were no children, and the trees forgot to blossom. Once a beautiful flower put its head out from the grass, but when it saw the notice-board it was so sorry for the children that it slipped back into the ground again, and went off to sleep. The only people who were pleased were the Snow and the Frost. 'Spring has forgotten this garden,' they cried, 'so we will live here all the year round.' The Snow covered up the grass with her great white cloak, and the Frost painted all the trees silver. Then they invited the North Wind to stay with them, and he came. He was wrapped in furs, and he roared all day about the garden, and blew the chimney-pots down. 'This is a delightful spot,' he said, 'we must ask the Hail on a visit.' So the Hail came. Every day for three hours he rattled on the roof of the castle till he broke most of the slates, and then he ran round and round the garden as fast as he could go. He was dressed in grey, and his breath was like ice.

'I cannot understand why the Spring is so late in coming,' said the Selfish Giant, as he sat at the window and looked out at his cold, white garden; 'I hope there will be a change in the weather.'

But the Spring never came, nor the Summer. The Autumn gave golden fruit to every garden, but to the Giant's garden she gave none. 'He is too selfish,' she said. So it was always Winter there, and the North Wind and the Hail, and the Frost, and the Snow danced about through the trees.

One morning the Giant was lying awake in bed when he

heard some lovely music. It sounded so sweet to his ears that he thought it must be the King's musicians passing by. It was really only a little linnet singing outside his window, but it was so long since he had heard a bird sing in his garden that it seemed to him to be the most beautiful music in the world. Then the Hail stopped dancing over his head, and the North Wind ceased roaring, and a delicious perfume came to him through the open casement. 'I believe the Spring has come at last,' said the Giant; and he jumped out of bed and looked out.

What did he see?

He saw a most wonderful sight. Through a little hole in the wall the children had crept in, and they were sitting in the branches of the trees. In every tree that he could see there was a little child. And the trees were so glad to have the children back again that they had covered themselves with blossoms, and were waving their arms gently above the children's heads. The birds were flying about and twittering with delight, and the flowers were looking up through the green grass and laughing. It was a lovely scene, only in one corner it was still winter. It was the farthest corner of the garden, and in it was standing a little boy. He was so small that he could not reach up to the branches of the tree, and he was wandering all round it, crying bitterly. The poor tree was still quite covered with frost and snow, and the North Wind was blowing and roaring above it. 'Climb up! little boy,' said the Tree, and it bent its branches down as low as it could; but the boy was too tiny.

And the Giant's heart melted as he looked out. 'How selfish I have been!' he said; 'now I know why the Spring would not come here. I will put that poor little boy on the top of the tree, and then I will knock down the wall, and my garden shall be the children's playground for ever and ever.' He was really very sorry for what he had done.

So he crept downstairs and opened the front door quite

softly, and went out into the garden. But when the children saw him they were so frightened that they all ran away, and the garden became winter again. Only the little boy did not run, for his eyes were so full of tears that he did not see the Giant coming.

And the Giant stole up behind him and took him gently in his hand, and put him up into the tree. And the tree broke at once into blossom, and the birds came and sang on it, and the little boy stretched out his two arms and flung them round the Giant's neck, and kissed him. And the other children, when they saw that the Giant was not wicked any longer, came running back, and with them came the Spring. 'It is your garden now, little children,' said the Giant, and he took a great axe and knocked down the wall. And when the people were going to market at twelve o'clock they found the Giant playing with the children in the most beautiful garden they had ever seen.

All day long they played, and in the evening they came to the Giant to bid him good-bye.

'But where is your little companion?' he said: 'the boy I put into the tree.' The Giant loved him the best because he had kissed him.

'We don't know,' answered the children: 'he has gone away.'

'You must tell him to be sure and come tomorrow,' said the Giant. But the children said that they did not know where he lived, and had never seen him before; and the Giant felt very sad.

Every afternoon, when school was over, the children came and played with the Giant. But the little boy whom the Giant loved was never seen again. The Giant was very kind to all the children, yet he longed for his first little friend, and often spoke of him. 'How I would like to see him!' he used to say.

Years went over, and the Giant grew very old and feeble.

He could not play about any more, so he sat in a huge arm-chair, and watched the children at their games, and admired his garden. 'I have many beautiful flowers,' he said; 'but the children are the most beautiful flowers of all.'

One winter morning he looked out of his window as he was dressing. He did not hate the Winter now, for he knew that it was merely the Spring asleep, and that the flowers were resting.

Suddenly he rubbed his eyes in wonder and looked and looked. It certainly was a marvellous sight. In the farthest corner of the garden was a tree quite covered with lovely white blossoms. Its branches were all golden, and silver fruit hung down from them, and underneath it stood the little boy he had loved.

Downstairs ran the Giant in great joy, and out into the garden. He hastened across the grass, and came near to the child. And when he came quite close his face grew red with anger, and he said, 'Who hath dared to wound thee?' For on the palms of the child's hands were the prints of two nails, and the prints of two nails were on the little feet.

'Who hath dared to wound thee?' cried the Giant; 'tell me, that I may take my big sword and slay him.'

'Nay!' answered the child: 'but these are the wounds of Love.'

'Who art thou?' said the Giant, and a strange awe fell on him, and he knelt before the little child.

And the child smiled on the Giant, and said to him, 'You let me play once in your garden, today you shall come with me to my garden, which is Paradise.'

And when the children ran in that afternoon, they found the Giant lying dead under the tree, all covered with white blossoms.

From *The Complete Fairy Tales of Oscar Wilde* (Bodley Head, London, and Watts, N.Y.)

(See Note, page 213)

Suppose You Met a Witch

Suppose you met a witch . . . There's one I know,
all willow-gnarled and whiskered head to toe.
We drownded her at Ten Foot Bridge
last June, I think,—
but I've seen her often since at twilight time
under the willows by the river brink,
skimming the wool-white meadow mist
astride her broom o'beech.
And once, as she flew past, with a sudden twist
and flick of the stick she whisked me in
head over heels, splash in the scummy water
up to my chin —
ugh! . . .
Yet there are witless folk will say
they don't exist.
But I was saying—suppose *you* met a witch,
up in that murky waste of wood
where you play your hide and seek. Suppose
she pounced from out a bush,
she touched you, she clutched you,
what would you do? No use
in struggling, in vain to pinch and pull.
She's pinned you down, pitched you into her sack,
drawn tight the noose.

There's one way
of escape, one word you need to know—
W – A – N – D. Well,
what does that spell? . . .

They learnt it years ago,
two children—Roland and Miranda—clapped
in a witch's sack and trapped
just as you might be. *He*
was a mild and dreamy boy, musical
as a lark—in the dark
of the jolting sack he sang. *She*
was quick in all she did, a nimble wit, her brain
busy as a hive of bees at honey time.

And Grimblegrum—that was the witch's name—
jogged them home.

This was the usual sort, a candy villa
with walls of gingerbread, porch and pillar
of barley sugar. She kicked the gate
and the licorice-beaded door,
undid the sack string and tipped them
on the glassy glacier-minted floor.
As Roland fell, his boot struck
the crystal paving stones and chipped them.
Like an angry rocket
she launched at him. Miranda
sprang for the magic wand
and pinched it from her pocket.

> 'Tip, tap—O house of cake,
> be a cloud-reflecting lake
> with me and Roland, each a swan,
> gracefully afloat thereon!
> And, deeper than e'er plummet sounded
> Grimblegrum the witch be drownded!'

'Twas done—look there, d'you see two swans
a-gliding, serene and cool

upon that heaven-painted pool,
over the blue sky, over the floating clouds that shine
like snow-white fleeces?
Sudden, in burst of bubbles the witch popped up
and shivered the clouds to pieces.
'I'll gobble you yet!' she gulped,
but all she gobbled was water as with windmill arms
she thrashed and lashed at them. No swimmer,
she would have sunk like a boulder below,
had not a felon crow,
black-hearted as his feather, swooping, dipping,
hoisted her by the belt and borne her, boggy,
drooping, dripping,
home.
          'She'll follow us—no time to lose—
quick, we must fly!' Miranda cried.
Heavily they rose;
far over field and forest, with whining wing
all night through
till dawn of day they flew.

Meanwhile the Grimble-witch, now dry,
had put on her seven league boots and (do or die)
seven mile at a step came galloping,
gulping, 'Gobble you yet, I'll gobble you yet!'

The swans heard her cackle, and a thudding where she
    stepped—
down by a screen of trees they swept,
down to a lonely roadside out of view.
          'I'll change myself to a rose of crimson hue,
set in a prickly hedge,' Miranda said,
'and, Roland, as for you,
you'll be a piper, and the magic wand
your flute.'

Not a second too soon—for the witch's boot
touched ground beside them. And she croaked:

'O glorious goriest rose!
I have sought you from afar,
how I wonder what you are!
You may mock me from on high,
but I'm the spider, you're the fly!
Ha! ha! ha! ha! ha!'

And she gaped at that glorious and goriest of roses
with the greediest of eyes and the nosiest of noses.
Again she spoke:
'Good piper, this rose—how dainty it would look
if I stuck it in my cloak!
May I pluck it?'
                    'Good lady, you may. And I'll play
to you the while.' And Roland smiled,
for his was a *magic* flute,
each golden note entrancing—
none could listen without dancing.

                    One note one,
                she spun like a top.

                    Two notes two,
            she hopped and couldn't stop.

                Three notes three—
        and into that thorny thistle-y tree
        with a hop, skip and a jump went she.

Tootle-toot! sang the flute
and up went her boot
and down again soon

to the tantivy tune.
Every thorn and twig
did dance to the jig
and the witch willy-nilly—
each prickle and pin
as it skewered her in
was driving her silly.

Hi!
   ho!
      shrieked she,
and *tickle-me-thistle!* and *prickle-de-dee!*
And battered she was as she trotted and tripped,

and her clothes were torn and tattered and ripped
till at last,
all mingled and mangled,

her right leg entangled,
    her left leg right-angled,
firm as a prisoner pinned to the mast,
she
      stuck
           fast.

Silence, not a sound as Roland wiped
the sweat from his brow. Then gently with his pipe
he touched the rose. Out leapt Miranda
to the ground. Hand in hand,
chuckling, through the wild wood
away home they ran.

That same evening, a cowman passing by
paused by a roadside bush to cut a switch.
He heard a cry;
turning, saw in a hedge nearby a prickly witch
who screamed and yelled and hissed at him and spat.

So he put a match to the hedge. And that was that.

From *Belinda and the Swans* by Ian Serraillier (Jonathan Cape, London)

(See Note, page 213)

The Monster Who Grew Small

Far to the South, beyond the Third Cataract, there was a small village, where a certain boy lived with his uncle. The uncle was known as the Brave One, because he was a hunter and killed such a lot of large animals; and he was very horrid to his nephew, because he thought the boy was a coward. He tried to frighten him by telling stories of the terrible monsters which he said lived in the forest; and the boy believed what he was told, for was not his uncle called the Brave One, the Mighty Hunter?

Whenever the boy had to go down to the river, he thought that crocodiles would eat him; and when he went into the forest, he thought that the shadows concealed snakes, and that hairy spiders waited under the leaves to pounce on him. The place which always felt specially dangerous was on the path down to the village; and whenever he had to go along it he used to run.

One day, when he came to the most frightening part of this path, he heard a voice crying out from the shadows of the darkest trees. He put his fingers in his ears and ran even faster; but he could still hear the voice. His fear was very loud, but even so he could hear his heart, and it said to him:

'Perhaps the owner of that voice is much more frightened than you are. You know what it feels like to be frightened: don't you think you ought to help?'

So he took his fingers out of his ears, and clenched his fists to make himself feel braver, and plunged into the deep shade, thrusting his way between thorn-trees in the direction of the cries.

He found a hare, caught by the leg in a tangle of creepers,

and the hare said to him, 'I was so very frightened: but now you have come I am not afraid any more. You must be very brave to come alone into the forest.'

The boy released the hare, and quietened it between his hands, saying, 'I am not at all brave. In my village they call me Miobi, the Frightened One. I should never have dared to come here, only I heard you calling.'

The Hare said to him, 'Why are you frightened? What are you frightened of?'

'I am frightened of the crocodiles who live in the river; and of the snakes, and the spiders, which lie in wait for me whenever I go out. But most of all I am frightened of the Things which rustle in the palm-thatch over my bed-place—my uncle says they are only rats and lizards, but I know they are far worse than that.'

'What you want,' said the Hare, 'is a house with walls three cubits thick, where you could shut yourself away from all the things you fear.'

'I don't think that would do any good,' said Miobi. 'For if there were no windows I should be afraid of not being able to breathe; and if there *were* windows I should always be watching them, waiting for Things to creep in to devour me.'

The Hare seemed to have stopped being frightened, and Miobi said to it, 'Now you know that I am not at all brave I don't suppose I'll seem much of a protection, but if you feel I'd be better than nothing I'll carry you home; if you'll tell me where you live.'

To Miobi's astonishment, the Hare replied, 'I live in the Moon, so you can't come home with me, yet. But I should like to give you something to show how grateful I am for your kindness. What would you like to have best in the world?'

'I should like to have Courage . . . But I suppose that's one of the things which can't be given.'

'I can't *give* it to you, but I can tell you where to find it. The road which leads there you will have to follow alone, but when your fears are strongest, look up to the Moon and I will tell you how to overcome them.'

Then the Hare told Miobi about the road he must follow, and the next morning, before his uncle was awake, the boy set out on his journey. His only weapon was a dagger which the Hare had given him; it was long and keen, pale as moon-light.

Soon the road came to a wide river: then Miobi was very frightened, for in it there floated many crocodiles, who watched him with their evil little eyes. But he remembered what the Hare had told him, and after looking up to the Moon, he shouted at them:

'If you want to be killed come and attack me!'

Then he plunged into the river, his dagger clutched in his hand, and began to swim to the far bank.

Much to the crocodiles' surprise, they found themselves afraid of him. To try to keep up their dignity, they said to each other, 'He is too thin to be worth the trouble of eating!' And they shut their eyes and pretended not to notice him. So Miobi crossed the river safely and went on his way.

After a few more days he saw two snakes, each so large that it could have swallowed an ox without getting a pain. Both speaking at the same time, they said loudly, 'If you come one step further we shall immediately eat you.'

Miobi was very frightened, for snakes were one of the things he minded most. He was on the point of running away, when he looked up to the Moon, and immediately knew what the Hare wanted him to do.

'O Large and Intelligent Serpents,' he said politely, 'a boy so small as myself could do no more than give *one* of you a satisfactory meal; half of me would not be worth the trouble of digesting. Hadn't you better decide between your-selves by whom I am to have the honour of being eaten?'

'Sensible, very. I will eat you myself,' said the first serpent.

'No, you won't, he's mine,' said the second.

'Nonsense, you had that rich merchant. He was so busy looking after his gold that he never noticed you, until you got him by the legs.'

'Well, what about the woman who was admiring her face in a mirror? You said she was the tenderest meal you'd had for months.'

'The merchant was *since* that,' said the first serpent firmly.

'He wasn't.'

'He was.'

'Wasn't!'

'Was!!'

While the serpents were busy arguing which of them should eat Miobi, he had slipped past without their noticing, and was already out of sight. So that morning neither of the serpents had even a small breakfast.

Miobi felt so cheerful that he began to whistle. For the first time, he found himself enjoying the shapes of trees and the colours of flowers, instead of wondering what dangers they might be concealing.

Soon he came in sight of a village, and even in the distance he could hear a sound of lamentation. As he walked down the single street no one took any notice of him, for the people were too busy moaning and wailing. The cooking-fires were unlit, and goats were bleating because no one had remembered to milk them. Babies were crying because they were hungry, and a small girl was yelling because she had fallen down and cut her knee and her mother wasn't even interested. Miobi went to the house of the Headman, whom he found sitting cross-legged, with ashes on his head, his eyes shut, and his fingers in his ears.

Miobi had to shout very loud to make him hear. Then the old man opened one ear and one eye, and growled, 'What do you want?'

'Nothing,' said Miobi politely; 'I wanted to ask what *you* wanted. Why is your village so unhappy?'

'You'd be unhappy,' said the Headman crossly, 'if you were going to be eaten by a Monster.'

'Who is going to be eaten? You?'

'Me and everyone else, even the goats; can't you hear them bleating?'

Miobi was too polite to suggest that the goats were only bleating because no one had milked them. So he asked the Headman, 'There seems to be quite a lot of people in your village; couldn't you kill the Monster if you all helped?'

'Impossible!' said the Headman. 'Too big, too fierce, too terrible. We are *all* agreed on that.'

'What does the Monster look like?' asked Miobi.

'They say it has the head of a crocodile, and the body of a hippopotamus, and a tail like a very fat snake, but it's sure to be even worse. Don't talk about it!' He put his hands over his face and rocked backwards and forwards, moaning to himself.

'If you will tell me where the Monster lives, I will try to kill it for you,' said Miobi, much to his own surprise.

'Perhaps you are wise,' said the Headman, 'for then you will be eaten first and won't have so long to think about it. The Monster lives in the cave on the top of that mountain. The smoke you can see comes from his fiery breath, so you'll be cooked before you are eaten.'

Miobi looked up to the Moon and he knew what the Hare wanted him to say, so he said it. 'I will go up the mountain and challenge the Monster.'

Climbing the mountain took him a long time; but when he was half-way up, he could see the Monster quite clearly. Basking at the mouth of its cave, its fiery breath wooshing out of its nostrils, it looked about three times as big as the Royal Barge—which is very big, even for a monster.

Miobi said to himself, 'I won't look at it again until I have climbed all the distance between me and the cave; otherwise I might feel too much like running away to be able to go on climbing.'

When next he looked at the Monster, he expected it to be much larger than it had seemed from further away. But instead it looked quite definitely smaller, only a little bigger than one Royal Barge instead of three. The Monster saw him. It snorted angrily, and the snort flared down the mountain-side and scorched Miobi: he ran back rather a long way before he could make himself stop. Now the Monster seemed to have grown larger again; it was *quite* three times as large as the Royal Barge—perhaps four.

Miobi said to himself, 'This is very curious indeed: the further I run away from the Monster, the larger it seems, and the nearer I am to it, the smaller it seems. Perhaps if I was *very* close it might be a reasonable size for me to kill with my dagger.'

So that he would not be blinded by the fiery breath, he shut his eyes; and so that he would not drop his dagger, he clasped it very tightly; and so that he would not have time to start being frightened, he ran as fast as he could up the mountain to the cave.

When he opened his eyes he couldn't see anything which needed killing. The cave seemed empty, and he began to think that he must have run in the wrong direction. Then he felt something hot touch his right foot: he looked down, and there was the Monster—and it was as small as a frog! He picked it up in his hand and scratched its back. It was no more than comfortably warm to hold, and it made a small, friendly sound, half-way between a purr and the simmer of a cooking-pot.

Miobi thought, 'Poor little Monster! It will feel so lonely in this enormous cave.' Then he thought, 'It might make a nice pet, and its fiery breath would come in useful for lighting my cooking-fire.' So he carried it carefully down the mountain, and it curled up in his hand and went to sleep.

When the villagers saw Miobi, at first they thought they must be dreaming, for they had been so sure the Monster would kill him. Then they acclaimed him as a hero, saying,

'Honour to the mighty hunter! He, the bravest of all! He, who has slain the Monster!'

Miobi felt very embarrassed, and as soon as he could make himself heard above the cheering, he said, 'But I didn't kill it; I brought it home as a pet.'

They thought that was only the modesty becoming to a hero, and before they would believe him he had to explain how the Monster had only seemed big so long as he was running away, and that the nearer he got to it the smaller it grew, until at last, when he was standing beside it, he could pick it up in his hand.

The people crowded round to see the Monster. It woke up, yawned a small puff of smoke, and began to purr. A little girl said to Miobi, 'What is its name?'

'I don't know,' said Miobi, 'I never asked it.'

It was the Monster himself who answered her question. He stopped purring, looked round to make sure everyone was listening, and then said:

'I have many names. Some call me Famine, and some Pestilence; but the most pitiable of humans give me their own names.' It yawned again, and then added, 'But most people call me, What-Might-Happen.'

From *The Scarlet Fish and Other Stories* by Joan Grant (Methuen, London)

(See Note, page 214)

The Children of Lir

In the far off days when the gods lived in Ireland, Bov the Red was their King. He had two foster daughters and Lir, father of the sea god, sought one of them in marriage.

The marriage was happy and Lir's wife bore him four children, a daughter named Fionuala, 'Maid of the fair shoulder', a son Aed and twin boys, Fiacra and Conn. But with the twins' birth, their sweet mother died and great was Lir's grief.

After a time Lir asked for Bov's second foster-daughter, Aeife, as his wife, so that his children might have a mother again. Aeife was very beautiful and at first she loved her stepchildren. But as the years went by and they grew in beauty and charm, Aeife began to look at them with a jealous eye. She had no child of her own and she felt that her husband loved his children better than he loved her. Evil grows when it is a close companion, and soon Aeife began to hate the children and to long to be rid of them.

One day she called the four to her and told them that she would take them on a visit to their grandfather, Bov the Red. With shouts of glee the children sprang into the chariot and away galloped the horses in the bright sunshine. But as they approached a wild and lonely place where lay Lake Derry-varagh, Aeife stopped the chariot and drew the driver on one side and commanded him to kill the children. Although she offered him untold riches, the man refused to do so wicked a deed. Nor would any of her servants do her bidding.

Then, pretending that it had only been a test of their loyalty, Aeife, with a false smile, took the children with her to the edge of the lake and laughingly sent them into the water to bathe. 'Come,' she said, 'the water is warm and you are hot with the journey. Play in the shallows for a while.'

The three boys threw off their clothes and jumped into the water with a splash and a shout. But Fionuala drew back for she did not trust her stepmother. Then, seeing her brothers playing together, she too waded into the water to join them.

Then Aeife took a magic wand from beneath her dark cloak and, crying out an incantation in loud tones, she changed the children into four white swans.

But Aeife had forgotten one thing. Although she could take away their human shape, she could not deprive them of their human hearts and their human speech. So now Fionuala swam to the edge of the reedy lake and cried out: 'Give us back our human shape, stepmother! Our father will die of grief if he loses his children.'

Aeife's heart was so full of jealousy that she would not listen. In a loud voice she chanted the children's terrible doom:

'For three hundred years you shall float on the waters of Lake Derryvaragh, for three hundred years on the Straits of Moyle, for three hundred years on the Atlantic by Erris and the Isle of Glora. When a woman from the South marries a man from the North, then—and only then—shall your enchantment end.'

Then the four snow-white swans huddled together in terror and begged her to set them free from such a fate, but Aeife turned away scornfully and rode on towards her father's house, telling the servants that the children had been drowned.

As well as their human speech, the children had kept their power to make sweet music, and now as they floated on the waters of the lake in the golden evening light, they began to sing softly so that their father, Lir, riding in search of them, heard that sad music and came to the edge of the water to listen.

Great was his sorrow when Fionuala told him of the fate that had come to them. 'Save us, father!' she cried.

'I want to run again and to feel the soft grass beneath my feet,' sighed Conn, the youngest of the brothers. 'Release us quickly from the enchantment, dear father.'

'Alas!' said his father. 'I have no magic strong enough.'

'Grieve not for us then, father,' said Fionuala. 'Only come each day and talk to your children and we will sing to you until you forget your grief.'

Frantic with sorrow and anger, Lir rushed to the palace of Bov the Red and demanded that his wife, Aeife, should be put to death. An even more terrible fate awaited her, for Bov changed her into a demon of the air and condemned her to fly for ever in the heart of the tempest. And there she flies to this day, her wickedness clothed in a demon's shape until the end of the world shall come.

But the swans sang on, so sweetly that people came from near and far to hear them sing. For three hundred years the land of Ireland was at peace and men and women spoke gently to each other because of the singing of the Children of Lir.

And so the first three hundred years drew to an end and one day the four swans bade their father farewell and rose into the air on their strong wings. Far away they flew, as was their fate, to the wild cliffs and stormy waters of Moyle. They had no friends there and the air was full of wild winds and shrieking seagulls. Forbidden by their enchantment to land, they were compelled to swim on the angry waters and to rest at night in clefts of the black cliffs. So cold was it that on winter nights of snow their feathers froze to the rocks. Sometimes the storm drove them apart and long hours passed before they could find each other again. But when things were at their worst, Fionuala would gather her brothers to her, Conn on her right hand, Fiacra on her left and Aed against her breast, and shelter them with her plumage.

At last the second three hundred years came to an end and the swans flew towards the wild Isle of Glora. On the way they passed once more over their old home, the Hill of the White Field. Nothing could they see there but green mounds and whin bushes and nettles, for, unknown to them, the gods had been defeated and had made themselves invisible. The eyes of the Children of Lir were sealed so that they could no longer see their father and his people feasting in the fairy palaces, forever young and handsome. So sadly the four swans flew on to their place of banishment, singing sorrowfully as they went.

On the wild Isle of Glora they made one friend, Evric the farmer, and to him they told their story and he it was who told it to others and so to me.

It came to pass that on a day of autumn sunshine when the trees were aflame with red and gold leaves, the thin and dreadful peal of a bell startled them from their sorrow. To them this music, so different from the fairy sounds they knew, was an ugly and terrifying sound. It came from a tiny reed hut on the shore at the doorway of which stood a man with a gentle face.

Timidly Fionuala and her brothers alighted at his feet, for they felt a compulsion to draw near him.

He greeted them kindly. 'Welcome, Children of Lir,' he said, 'for by your sweet singing I know you well.'

'If you know of our fate, change us back into our human shape by your magic!' the swans entreated him.

'I have no magic, children,' answered the hermit gently. 'I can only tell you of one greater than myself who will bring you to peace at last.'

Day after day the swans visited the hermit and listened as he told them of this new God, until their hearts were moved and they joined him in his praises and forgot their wrongs and found peace.

But the last part of their long and weary enchantment was still to come. It so happened that a Princess of Munster, a 'woman of the South', had married a Chieftain of the North. Hearing of the wonderful singing swans, she demanded that her husband bring them to her as a wedding gift.

Haughtily the Chieftain came to the hermit and ordered that the swans should be given to him. The hermit refused. The Chieftain offered him money and jewels to build a fine church, but still the hermit refused. 'I do not sell souls for money,' he said firmly. 'You shall not mock at these helpless children for your selfish pleasure.'

Filled with anger, the Chieftain seized the swans by their silver chains and dragged them to the palace.

Proudly the Princess sat on her throne. 'Sing!' she commanded. But suddenly her face grew pale with horror, for before her eyes the plumage fell from the swans. There stood a frail old woman and three feeble old men, so old that no man could tell how old they might be.

Swiftly the hermit came to bid farewell to his four friends and to bless them with a Christian blessing ere they died.

Then Fionuala spoke faintly: 'Lay us in one grave, I pray you, Conn at my right hand, Fiacra at my left and Aed against my breast. So have we rested so many times in pain and sorrow, so will we rest for ever.'

Thus was the death of the Children of Lir and the end of their long and sorrowful journey. They are gone, but their story is not forgotten, for do I not tell it to you again today?

Traditional, adapted by Eileen Colwell

(See Note, page 215)

The Magic Tea-Kettle

Once upon a time there was a temple in Japan, where a priest lived with a number of young men who were learning how to be priests, too. It was a very pretty temple on the side of a hill where a little stream flowed. And in that stream there were silver fish and very clear sparkling water. Every morning the priest used to go there to fill his kettle so as to make tea, and catch a little fish on the end of a rod.

One day, when he had caught his fish as usual, and filled his kettle, he was climbing up the hill and back to the temple, when he felt what *he* thought were drops of rain on his foot. He looked up at the sky, but there were no clouds, and he felt nothing on his face. He listened. 'Drip-drip-drip!' 'Drop-drop-drop!' then faster, 'Drip-drop! Drip-drop!' His foot was getting quite wet. He could not understand it. Suddenly he looked at his kettle and saw that it was only half full. It was leaking, leaking all round the edge. Somebody must have been careless and knocked it against something sharp, then hung it up in the temple without telling the priest.

'Tut, tut, tut!' said the priest crossly. 'Now I shall have to fill another kettle, and I don't believe I've got one.'

He climbed the hill as quickly as he could, hoping to save some of the water, but when he reached the temple, the kettle was empty and he could not have any tea. He felt rather tired after his walk, but he knew that the others would want some tea, so he began to hunt about for a kettle. At first he could not find one anywhere, but at last he remembered that, hanging on a hook high up in a corner, was a very, very old one, an earthenware kettle which had been there for years and years and years. In fact, nobody had ever

known the time when it had not been there, and that is
really why the priest had forgotten it. He was so used to it.

'Well, well, well!' said he. 'Fancy my forgetting you—
when you've been there all these years! Come along!' He
climbed on to a stool, unhooked the kettle, blew a cloud of
dust off the top of it and once again set out for the stream.

It took him a little time to come home, because he had to
wash the kettle before filling it. Also it was a good bit bigger
than the other one, so it was rather heavy. Naturally the
priest was quite glad to get back to the temple.

He sat on a reed mat on the floor and thought, 'Now for a
good cup of tea!'

He blew up the charcoal embers on the hearth, fixed up a
little three-legged arrangement on which he used to stand his
kettle, and began to boil the water.

And *then* something happened!

Please don't laugh, because really it was very serious. *The
kettle grew a tail!* Umm, I'm not joking! A great big hairy
one. It sprouted out of the side where the spout came, and
began to move very slowly backwards and forwards. Wiggle-
waggle! Wiggle-waggle! The priest was simply terrified. At
first he thought that something had gone wrong with his own
sight. He rubbed his eyes and looked again, and there was
the kettle going bubble-bubble, bubble-bubble, and the tail
going wiggle-waggle, wiggle-waggle. 'Ay yi-yi!' shouted the
priest. 'Help! Help!'

There was a patter-patter-patter of bare feet across the
bamboo floor, and in ran one of the priest's pupils. 'Oh dear!
Oh dear! What *has* happened?' asked the pupil. 'Are you
ill, dear master?' But the priest could do nothing but point
weakly at the kettle and whimper, 'He's got a t-t-tail!' Then
all the priest's pupils came running in and looked at the
kettle and began to scream at once. One cried, 'Oh-oh!' Another cried, 'Ah-ah!' and another, 'Ee-ee!' and another,
'Ii-Ii!' You've never heard such a clatter in your lives; and

all the time the tail went slowly to and fro, wiggle-waggle, wiggle-waggle.

The priest's pupils were pale with horror, but just as they were calming down and wondering what to do, a change came over the kettle. The tail went faster, wiggle-waggle, wiggle-waggle, wiggle-waggle! The water inside boiled furiously, bubble-bubble-bubble, and on the side opposite the tail a large crack suddenly appeared.

What?

No, it was not water which came out, b-but, well, I hardly like to tell you, it was a nose! And after the nose came the whole head. A hairy head with brown beady eyes and sharp white teeth. It was the head of a badger.

Now, I ask you, what would you do with a kettle which had a hairy tail and a badger's head?

Of course, the priest and all his pupils began to scream again. You should have heard them Ah-ahing and Ee-ee-ing and Ii-ii-ing and Oh-ohing! Really, they might have been in the Zoo instead of a Japanese temple. I believe it frightened the kettle, I mean the badger—no, what do I mean? The badger-kettle! The water went bubble-bubble, and the tail went wiggle-waggle, and the teeth went snip-snap, and that kettle jumped clean off the fire and began careering round the room. Whee-oo! It was awful. 'Oh-oh! Ah-ah! Ee-ee! Ii-Ii!' How those young men squealed and how they ran! 'Catch it by the tail!' cried one. 'Catch it yourself!' cried another. I can't tell you what a racket there was. On went the kettle rampaging round the room with its tail sticking out behind, and its badger's head sticking out in front, and the steam from the water inside lifting the lid up and down, up and down in the most uncanny way. And all the young men squealing like pigs and throwing things at it. And, would you believe it? They missed it every time. At last they grew so tired of running about and throwing things that they began to make a proper plan. One of them went outside and found a rope. The others all joined hands, and very carefully they followed the kettle's movements, creeping closer and closer until they managed to drive it into a corner. Then with a shout, 'Whoo-up!' one of them threw the rope and caught the kettle in a slip knot. Well, naturally all the water was spilt. But the teeth went on snapping and the tail went on waggling, and it took them quite ten minutes to tie up that poor old kettle and shut it into a box.

When it was over they were simply exhausted, and even then they could not have any tea, because, of course, they had not anything to boil the water in. They all sat down feeling very sorry for themselves. Presently there came a tap at the door, and they heard the voice of a tinker crying, 'Have you any old rubbish for sale? Any old knives or pails or kettles?'

Kettles! The priest and his pupils looked at one another. Very softly one of them stole tiptoe to the box and peeped in! There was the kettle lying quite quietly at the bottom of the box, and lo and behold! the tail and the head had disappeared.

One by one the priest and his pupils came up and looked at it, and all the time the old tinker was tapping at the door and crying, 'Any old rubbish for sale? Any old knives, pails or kettles?'

'Come in!' said the priest. 'I have got an old kettle here! Do you want to buy it? I'll sell it cheap!' All the pupils began to shiver and shake. They were terrified lest the awful tail and head should suddenly sprout again, and they did so want to get rid of the kettle. They thought it was a hobgoblin.

The tinker, little guessing what had happened, picked up the kettle and looked at it. He undid the knots of the rope, and all the priest's pupils gibbered with fright. 'It's a dusty old thing,' said the tinker, 'but I dare say I shall find it useful. Here you are! I can't give you more than that for it.' He put three little coins into the priest's hand and walked off with the kettle under his arm. And—and what *do* you think happened? That awful tail sprouted once more, waggled 'good-bye' to the priest and his pupils, and then popped in again.

Luckily the tinker did not see it or he might have returned the kettle and asked for his money back. Instead, he just trudged home and put the kettle in a corner among a lot of other rubbish. Then he pulled out a mat, curled himself up and went to sleep on the floor.

That night he woke up, hearing a little scratchy noise by his feet. He opened his eyes and there was the kettle which he had bought at the temple walking round the room on four furry legs! At one end there was the head of a badger with teeth snip-snapping, and at the other there was a long hairy tail going wiggle-waggle, wiggle-waggle. My goodness! the tinker *was* in such a fright. He leapt up with a start, but no sooner was he on his feet than the kettle was a kettle again, so he lay down feeling very much puzzled.

Of course, the same thing happened night after night until the poor tinker was quite worn out with the worry of it. You see, he was a kind soul. He kept thinking to himself, 'If the kettle's a badger it ought to be fed! And if the badger's a kettle it ought to be boiled.' He simply did not know what to do, so at last he consulted a friend. 'You come and see my kettle,' said he, 'and then you can tell me what to do.'

The friend came round that very night, and everything happened as before. The tail grew and waggled, the head of the badger snapped its teeth, and the kettle ran round on four furry legs.

'Well, you *are* silly!' said the tinker's friend; 'that's a magic kettle! It's lucky! I tell you what. You be a showman. You can teach your kettle to dance and walk on a tight-rope, holding up an umbrella, and then make people pay to come and see it. Why, you'll be rich for ever!'

And that's exactly what happened.

You should have seen that little kettle dancing! Snip-snap went the teeth, wiggle-waggle went the tail. One hairy paw held up a little paper umbrella, and two hairy paws danced in the most graceful way on a tight-rope. And the whole of Japan flocked to see the wonderful kettle.

In a very few years the tinker was so rich that he retired and gave lots of money to the poor.

And do you know what he did in the end? He gave the kettle back to the old priest and his pupils, and they made a special shelf for it and treated it with great respect.

But it never turned into a dancing badger again.

What do you say? Why? Oh, I don't know. I expect it was getting old, and you know when people get old they like to settle down and be quiet.

From *Stories from Everywhere* by Rhoda Power (Evans, London)

(See Note, page 215)

The Midnight Folk

When Kay got into bed, the sun was nearly down; a glow from it lit the wall opposite, so that the hunting men riding at the brook in Full Cry were made most vivid. A ray touched the model of the *Plunderer*, so that she glowed, too, and the green stripe upon her forecastle and the scarlet rims of her tops looked beautiful against her brown and black. 'I have had a jolly day,' he thought. 'And to-morrow, I'll jolly well go into the Crowmarsh Estate to see if I can't find the J. G. Z.'

Just before he fell asleep he was almost sure that the water in the brook in Full Cry had eddies in it; eddies, and those little clouds of dissolving earth which the water-rat makes when scared from a bank. 'He must have been a jolly good painter,' he thought, 'to be able to do all that.' He fell asleep soon after this, thinking that if he were a painter, he would paint, well, he did not know what he would paint; so very much was happening.

As before, he woke up into what seemed like broad daylight, although he could see the stars through the window. He was aware at once that something very odd was happening in the print of Full Cry: the hunting men, whose red coats were flapping, were turning from the brook. And what was the matter with the brook? It was very, very full of water, and coming with such a strong current that it swished against the loose alder root. He could see not only eddies, but bright, hurrying, gleaming ripples which ran into bubbles, and yes, yes, it was coming into the room, it was running on both sides of the bed, clear, swift, rushing water, carrying down petals and leaves and bits of twig. Then there came the water-rats, who dived with a phlumphing noise when they caught sight of him. He was on an island in the midst of the stream; and the stream was so crystal clear that he could see the fish in the shallows, flapping like water-plant leaves, and filmy as dead weeds.

But what on earth was happening to the model of the *Plunderer*? He could see that the water had reached her on the wall: she was afloat. She seemed to be alive with little tiny men, all busy with ropes. No, they were not men, they were little mice, 'water-mice, I suppose', he thought. Now she was coming across the stream to him; and how big she was, or, no, how little he was; he was no bigger than the water-mice. There she came slowly to the edge of the bed. She had flags flying, a Blue Peter at the fore, a house-flag, with three oreilles couped proper, on the main, and a red ensign at the peak. But lovelier than the flags were the decks, with the little doors, each with a shiny brass handle and real lock and key, opening to the cabins. Then there were real lifeboats ready for use. He could see the barrels and lockers in them marked 'Best Preserved Milk', 'Corned Beef', 'Ship's Bread', 'Pemmican', 'Raisins', 'Chocolate Cream', 'Turkish Delight', 'Split Peas', 'Currants', 'Hundreds and Thousands', 'Mixed Biscuits', 'Dry Ginger Beer', etc., etc. No fear of starving in lifeboats like those. Then all the little brass cannon were shining in the sun, ready for use, with the little powder tubs all handy, and little men standing by them ready to fire them off in salute. Then as the ship came alongside the bed, each little gunner blew puff upon his match, to make it glow (some of them had red-hot pokers instead of matches), just as the *Sea-Gunner's Practice* described, and popped the glowing end on the touchholes. All the little brass cannon went bang together in salute.

Then Kay saw that the captain of the ship was his friend the Water-Rat. He was standing on the poop, with his tele-scope in his hand, telling the mate to put the gangway over for Mr Kay. Some of the little seamen at once thrust out a gangway on to the bed.

'Step on board, Mr Kay,' the Captain said.

'May I really and truly?'

'Yes, we're waiting for you.'

Kay walked from his bed to the deck. He was amazed at the neatness of everything: all the rows of buckets, the sponges and rammers for the cannon, the capstans that worked, the compasses that pointed, the cask, painted red, for salt meat, and the other cask, painted blue, for fresh water; and all the rigging, with little ladders on it for going aloft. Then there was a ship's kitchen on the deck close to him, with a real little cook, with a wooden leg, making plum-duff for dinner at a real fire.

'Welcome on board, Mr Kay,' the Captain said. 'I thought we might stand over to the westward to see what we can find of the old *Plunderer*. We've got a cabin prepared for you, with a hammock slung to it; and here are some nice long sea-boots to pull over your pyjamas, and a double-breasted pea-jacket to keep out the seas and keep in the plum-duff. And now, my hearties, cast loose forward, let go aft. The tug has got her. Hurray, lads, for the westward.'

Kay noticed now, what he had not noticed before, that on the other side of the *Plunderer* was a tug-boat under steam. Long before, he had had a beautiful tug-boat with a scarlet funnel. She had gone by real steam made by methylated spirit, which you lit under the boiler in a little lamp. But after two voyages, she set forth across the Squire's pond on a windy day, and in the draught of the gale she caught fire, blazed for a few minutes from stem to stern, and then went down head first in deep water. Yet now here she was, re-painted, and with powerful new engines in her, which were threshing the water as they towed the *Plunderer* clear of the bed.

Soon they had swung round clear of the sofa, and headed

to the west, through the open window, into the night. Side
lights and towing lights were lit; she plunged on beside her
tug, casting streaks of coloured light upon the water. Soon
she was in the stream where Kay had so often seen the
Water Rat. Someone in the *Plunderer* turned a strong searchlight on to the water ahead. Look-out men went aloft to
watch the water: they called to the helmsman from time to
time to do this or that to dodge the rocks. 'A bit anxious,
this reach of the stream,' the Water Rat said, 'but there's
lots of water to-night.'

The ship went faster and faster over rapids and shallows:
soon she was in the big, quiet pool where the stream entered
the river. An otter looked out at them and wished them good
luck. A moorhen came out and swam ahead of them to show
them the best passage. Dawn was now breaking; but all the
world of men was asleep. Kay saw the deserted quay of the
river bank where he had so often watched people coming to
hire skiffs. A light was burning there, although morning was
growing everywhere. Kay saw the tug stand away from the
Plunderer's side and cast loose the tow-ropes. The *Plunderer*'s
men ran aloft and cast loose the sails. When Kay next looked
back, the river wharf was far astern; the ship was running
swiftly down the river under a press of sail.

'But come, Master Kay,' the Captain said, 'breakfast is on
the table. Step down the ladder with me to the cabin.'

He led the way down to a passage where there were a great
many doors labelled First Mate, Second Mate, Third Mate,
Captain's Stores, Instrument Room, Chart Room, Steward's
Pantry, Bullion Room, warranted iron-lined, Captain's Bath,
Mate's Bath, Jam Room, Sardine Room, etc., as well as one
big open door leading to the cabin, where the table was set
for breakfast. They had for breakfast all the things that Kay
was fondest of: very hot, little, round loaves of new white
bread baked in the embers of a wood-fire, very salt butter, a
sardine with a lot of olive oil, some minced kidneys, a poached

egg and frizzled bacon, a very fat sausage all bursting out of
its skin, a home-made pork-pie, with cold jelly and yolk of
egg beneath the crust, a bowl of strawberries and cream with
sifted sugar, a bowl of raspberries and cream with blobs of
sugar-candyish brown sugar that you could scrunch, some
nice new mushrooms and chicken, part of a honeycomb with
cream, a cup of coffee with crystals of white sugar candy for
a change, a yellow plum, a greengage and then a ripe blue
plum of Pershore to finish off with.

'That's the way, Master Kay,' the Captain said. 'I always
believe in a good breakfast: something to do your work on
and start the day with. And now, if you've finished, as you
haven't had much sleep lately, perhaps you'd like to keep
the next watch in your hammock. Come up on deck for a
moment first, though, we are now in the open sea.'

The wonder of it was that they *were* in the open sea, out of
sight of land, with the ship under full sail flying westward.
One or two of the water-mice were at work far aloft: others
on deck were washing their clothes and hanging them out to
dry on clothes-lines, or fishing with hooks and lines, or feed-
ing the sparrows (which they kept for the eggs) in the hen-
coops, or polishing the brass on the ship's bells and railings.
The sea was all blue and bright, the hot sun was shining,
not a cloud could be seen. The ship was flying faster and
faster.

Kay's cabin was a charming room, with mahogany lockers,
and a porthole covered with red curtains. A telescope hung on
a rack ready for use. A canvas hammock swung from hooks
in the wall, it had a pillow, mattress, sheets and blankets.
The Captain showed him how to get in and tuck himself up.
In a minute he was fast asleep.

He was wakened half an hour later by the ship anchoring
in calm water. On going on deck he found that she was not
far from a low, tropical shore, blindingly white, from the
surf bursting on it. Palm trees grew here and there on the

shore: there was no sign of man. The water, bright blue to seaward, with vivid green streaks, was clear as crystal.

'Now, Master Kay,' the Captain said, 'we will get into the diving-bell and go down to see what we can see. We are now just over the wreck of the old *Plunderer*.'

'How do you know?' Kay asked.

'We can always get directions about wrecks, we under-water folk,' the Captain said. 'We ask the otters, and they get into touch with all sorts of sea-folk, mermaids and sirens, not to speak of dolphins and these other fellows. Some of them are very old and have astonishing memories. It was a mermaid who told Tom Otter about the *Plunderer*, and he told me.'

The diving-bell was a tight little room, just big enough for two nice comfortable arm-chairs. It was built of iron framing, with floor and side windows of strong clear glass. Air-pipes and speaking-tubes were let into the walls and through the roof. When Kay and the Captain had taken their seats in the arm-chairs, the crew closed the door very carefully so that no water could possibly squeeze in. Then they hoisted the bell up and began to lower it carefully into the water. Kay found that he could see quite clearly through the glass of the sides and the floor. The fish came to the windows and sucked at them with their mouths. Presently, when the Captain called through the speaking-tube to stop lowering, he turned on a searchlight which pointed through the floor. Kay could see the bottom of the sea, growing like a garden with white and red coral, weeds, anemones and sponges, all seeming to dilate in the light. Some gaily-coloured fish came poking to the light, to find if it were good to eat; a few big fish, some of them like shadows, others like round collapsing bags with suckers waving from them, drifted or finned by, all noiseless; there was no whisper of sound, except a drumming in the ears. 'There's what is left of the *Plunderer*,' the Captain said.

Lying on the bottom, partly on white sand, partly among coral and weed, was the wreck of an old wooden ship. All that remained in sight of her was her stern post, her name-plate, marked *Plunderer*, a part of her keel, and a few ribs fallen out of place. All these timbers had been blackened by years under the sea. White and blue barnacles were growing on them; sprays of red and white coral had thrust up among them. The sunlight made all these things so glorious suddenly that the Captain turned out the light. Kay could see even the eyes of the lobsters peering into the crannies of the coral.

A mermaid floated to the side of the diving-bell. She was young and merry-looking, with bright, big brown eyes and very white teeth. She wore a gold crown over her long brown hair. Her cheeks and lips were full of colour. She put her mouth to the glass and smiled at them. 'That's Sea-Flower,' the Captain said. 'Say good morning to her.'

'Good morning, Miss Sea-Flower,' Kay said. 'Can you tell us how this ship came here?'

'Yes,' she said. 'She was upset in a squall, long ago, and all her men were drowned. They were making merry at the time. You can still see one of them: that scarlet coral is he. But open the door and come with me.'

Three other mermaids had swum to the diving-bell, to-gether they opened the door. In an instant, Kay was swim-ming with them in the warm water that was so like green light. All the floor of the sea shone. Here and there were patches of a green plant which had flowers like flames, they were so bright. At first he thought that everything there was dead; but when he had been twenty seconds in that tingling water he knew that it was full of life. The white sand of the sea-floor was alive with tiny, scurrying, glittering creatures, little beings looked at him from the branches of the coral, flowers poked out eyes at him upon stalks like snails' horns, he could see the leaves of the seaweeds shine with joy at every

good suck-in of light. All these living forms were swaying
gently as the swell lifted and fell: all were glistening and
tingling with joy; a kind of drowsy song of delight moved
through the water, everything was singing, or murmuring or
sighing because life was so good.

Kay went up to a big scarlet fish that had pale goggle-eyes
and a collapsing mouth; he tickled its throat; and others
knew that he was liking it, because they, too, came to have
their throats tickled, till he was surrounded by fish of all
colours and shapes, scaled and slimy, finned or legged, or
feelered, all noiseless, most of them strange, many of them
most beautiful.

'Come away, Kay,' the mermaids said. 'But first look at
the lovely golden lad.'

Lying among the coral, as though he were resting upon a
bank of flowers, was a golden image of Saint George, still
holding a white shield with a scarlet cross.

'We used to sing to him at first,' Sea-Flower said, 'hoping
that he would wake. The ship was full of golden and silver
people at one time. We loved them, they were so very
beautiful; but they never answered when we spoke to them.
Men came here searching for them in the old days, dragging
anchors for them along the sea-floor. At last some Indian
divers came down and carried them all away to a yacht, all
except this one, which they would not touch, because we had
so decked it with flowers.

'I see that you know who it was who took those lovely
things. He was going to take them to a city of evil men near
here. We followed his yacht on his way thither, for we were
sad to lose our lovely people. But come, Kay, you shall come
with us as far as we can go on the way those golden people
went.'

They all set out together, Kay between Sea-Flower and
Foam-Blossom, each of whom held one of his hands. Foam-
Blossom was a golden-haired mermaid, with bright blue eyes

and lovely rosy cheeks; she was always laughing. 'Is not this lovely?' she said, as they went swimming along.

'O, it *is* lovely,' Kay said. Every stroke of their arms took them over some new kind of shell-fish, or past some new anemone or waving weed.

'Come,' Sea-Flower said, 'let us go in on the tide, at the surface.'

They rose up together to the air. There, on the shallow shore, long lines of rollers were always advancing to the beach, toppling as they went and at last shattering. A little river came out to the sea there; its little waves seemed to enjoy meeting the big waves.

'Come,' Foam-Blossom said, 'let us ride on this big roller that is just going in.'

Together they sat on the neck of the wave, with Kay between them. Kay felt the wave begin to run like a horse, and to gather speed and to lift. Soon the toppling water began to hiss and foam all about them; the shore seemed to rush nearer, and then they all rolled over and over in boiling bubbles into the cool pool of the river, where the sea-shells looked as though they were all made of pearl.

Soon they were swimming up a river which flowed between ranks of reed and bulrush. Some of the reeds had flowers like the plumes of pampas grass, but pale blue; others had delicate, dangling, yellow tassels. All over these flowers the butterflies were hovering and settling. Giant flags grew among the reeds, with heavy blue, white and golden flowers. Little speckled birds with scarlet crests clung to these flowers while they pecked something within them. Water fowl as big as swans, with orange bills and big black and white plumes on their heads, swam to them to be stroked. In the gloom and zebra striping of the light and shade of the reeds Kay saw long-legged water birds standing ankle-deep, fishing. Here and there, when they passed mud-banks, he saw the turtles enjoying themselves in the cool ooze.

Presently they left the river and swam up a backwater, where the reeds on both sides gave place to quince-trees, which smelt like Arabia from the ripe fruit. At the end of the backwater there was a patch of red mud much poached by the feet of cows that had come to drink there. Beyond the cows was a little roll of grass-land.

'The man took the gold and silver things this way,' Sea-Flower said. 'In those days, the river ran this way, through all that grassy piece and for miles beyond it; we often used to swim there. We followed his yacht for a long way, further than we can see from here. He was a rosy-faced man, not old, but his hair was already grey; his eyes were very bright; and his mouth, when one could see it through the beard, was most cruel and evil. He had three Indians with him, who were his divers and sailors, whom he used to beat.

'When he was in a narrow part of the river, he heard guns, for his city of wickedness was being destroyed. He poled his yacht far into the reeds against the mud, and sent one of his Indians to find out what was happening. As the Indian did not come back, he sent a second Indian; and when the second did not come back he sent a third; but the third did not come back, either.'

'What happened to the Indians?' Kay asked.

'They all went home to their village in the sea; they have houses there, built upon piles driven into the water. In the rainy seasons they keep very snug in their hammocks and tell each other stories.'

'And what happened to Abner Brown, please?'

'He waited for the Indians to bring him news. When they did not come, he changed his yacht's hiding-place, by driving her still further into the reeds, and then he set out by himself to find out what was happening. He was captured as a pirate that same night and sent far away.

'Nobody found his boat, she was too well hidden, but there came great changes which hid her further. At first we used to play in the water near her, hoping that she might soon fall to pieces, so that we might have her gold and silver people again; but then there came the earthquake, which raised the river bed and buried the yacht in the mud. After the earthquake there came the great summer-floods, which made a new channel for the river and altered all the coast. When the floods went down, the place where the yacht lay was five miles from the water and covered deep with flowers, so the birds told us.

'The man came back presently to look for his yacht; but with the land so changed he hardly knew where to begin. We used to see him digging sometimes, when we went up the streams. But he was evil, do not let us think of him; let us go to the sea, to play in the rollers as they burst.'

In a few minutes they were in the shining shallow water across which the breaking rollers were marching. At first, Kay was frightened of the waves as they curled and toppled high over his head. Very soon he was wading to meet them, so that they could break all over him or carry him in to the sands.

'And now,' the mermaids said, 'let us all go down to look at the city under the sea.'

They all swam for a few minutes; then Kay suddenly saw something very golden in the green of the under-water.

'Those are the walls,' Foam-Blossom said. 'And if you listen, you will hear the bells. Let us wait here.'

They had paused at what had been the harbour. Three or four little ships had sunk with the city; they were there, still secured to the walls. Sponges like big yellow mushrooms covered one; another was starred all over with tiny white shells; another was thickly grown with a weed like many coloured ribbons. The walls, which had once been of white marble, seemed golden in that dim light. As Kay looked he heard a sweet but muffled booming of the bells as the swell of the water surged and lapsed in the bell-tower.

'Come, Kay,' the Sea-Flower said, 'the city gates have fallen open; we can go in.'

They passed through the gates, which now drooped upon their hinges from the weight of the shells which grew upon them. Inside the gates was a guard house, with a rack of spears still standing against the wall. Beyond that was a street, with shops open, and fish slowly finning from shop to shop. At the end of the street was a temple with a bell tower. No one was in that city. Kay went into two of the houses; in one, the kitchen was set out with pots and pans for dinner; two eggs were in a bowl and the bone of a leg of mutton was on a dish; in the other, the beds in the nursery were turned down ready for the children, and in one of the beds a child had set a doll, on which the little shells were growing. There were gaily painted carvings on some of the walls, showing the racing of children and romps and tugs-of-war.

'What is this city, please?' Kay asked. 'I would love to go all over it, into every house. What is it called?'

'We call it the Golden City. But look, here come the merchildren, playing Touch and Tag; let us play with them.'

At that instant, about twenty little merchildren came darting down the street, at full speed, with streaming hair, bright eyes and laughter. They twisted about like eels, dived down chimneys and through windows, crying aloud from joy in the fun.

'I wonder,' Kay said, 'if we might play Hide and Seek? This would be such a lovely place for it.'

'Yes,' Foam-Blossom said, 'let us all play Hide and Seek; Sea-Flower shall be He. And Kay, you come with me, for I know a lovely place to hide.'

She took him through one of the houses into what had been a garden. The fruit trees still stood, but were now crusted over with shells. Sponges, anemones and corals, which were so covered with points of glitter that they seemed full of eyes, grew like mistletoe on the branches. There came a sort of cloud in swift movement against the golden light.

'Look,' Foam-Blossom said, 'there's a ship passing over-head. If you look up, you may see one of the crew looking down.'

'That reminds me,' Kay asked, 'I meant to ask you before. Did you ever see another man taking away those golden and silver people? He may have taken them away in a big barge.'

'Why, Kay,' she answered, 'that is the *Plunderer* passing. There is the Water-Rat Captain looking down. You must be quick; and oh, do look at the flying fish.'

Kay felt a sort of swirl as he rushed past a lot of green bubbles into the light. The billows burst all about him suddenly and the sun made him blink. Foam-Blossom, the lovely merchildren, the city and its gardens, among which the beaked fishes had flitted like birds, were gone. He was sitting on the end of the *Plunderer*'s jib-boom in the clouds of spray flung up as she sailed. Sheets of spray, as bright as snow, soared and flashed all round him. Then he saw that it was not spray, but a flight of flying fish, skimming and falling like darts, all glittering and quivering. 'O, how lovely,' he cried.

As he cried, he heard his window creak; somebody rolled him into bed and the *Plunderer* went back to the wall. As for the sea, it was not there. When he opened his eyes, Ellen was there, but no water at all.

'Where did it all run to?' he asked.

'Where did what all run to? Wake up,' Ellen said. 'You are such a one to sleep as I never did.'

From *The Midnight Folk* by John Masefield (Heinemann, London, and Macmillan, N.Y.)

(See Note, page 216)

A Meal with a Magician

I have had some very odd meals in my time, and if I liked I could tell you about a meal in a mine, or a meal in Moscow, or a meal with a millionaire. But I think you will be more interested to hear about a meal I had one evening with a magician, because it is more unusual. People don't often have a meal of that sort, for rather few people know a magician at all well, because there aren't very many in England. Of course I am talking about real magicians. Some conjurors call themselves magicians, and they are very clever men. But they can't do the sort of things that real magicians do. I mean, a conjuror can turn a rabbit into a bowl of goldfish, but it's always done under cover or behind something, so that you can't see just what is happening. But a real magician can turn a cow into a grandfather clock with people looking on all the time. Only it is very much harder work, and no one could do it twice a day, and six days a week, like the conjurors do with rabbits.

When I first met Mr Leakey I never guessed he was a magician. I met him like this. I was going across the Hay-market about five o'clock one afternoon. When I got to the refuge by a lamp-post in the middle I stopped, but a little man who had crossed so far with me went on. Then he saw a motor-bus going down the hill and jumped back, which is al-ways a silly thing to do. He jumped right in front of a car, and if I hadn't grabbed his overcoat collar and pulled him back on to the refuge, I think the car would have knocked him down. For it was wet weather, and the road was very greasy, so it only skidded when the driver put the brakes on.

The little man was very grateful, but dreadfully frightened, so I gave him my arm across the street, and saw him back to his home, which was quite near. I won't tell you where it was, because if I did you might go there and bother him, and if he got really grumpy it might be very awkward indeed for you. I mean, he might make one of your ears as big as a cabbage-leaf, or turn your hair green, or exchange your right and left feet, or something like that. And then everyone who saw you would burst out laughing, and say, 'Here comes wonky Willie, or lop-sided Lizzie,' or whatever your name is.

'I can't bear modern traffic,' he said, 'the motor-buses make me so frightened. If it wasn't for my work in London I should like to live on a little island where there are no roads, or on the top of a mountain, or somewhere like that.' The little man was sure I had saved his life, and insisted on my having dinner with him, so I said I would come to dinner on Wednesday week. I didn't notice anything specially odd about him then, except that his ears were rather large and that he had a little tuft of hair on the top of each of them, rather like the lynx at the Zoo. I remember I thought if I had hair there I would shave it off. He told me that his name was Leakey, and that he lived on the first floor.

Well, on Wednesday week I went to dinner with him. I went upstairs in a block of flats and knocked at a quite ordinary door, and the little hall of the flat was quite ordinary too, but when I got inside it was one of the oddest rooms I have ever seen. Instead of wallpaper there were curtains round it, embroidered with pictures of people and animals. There was a picture of two men building a house, and another of a man with a dog and a cross-bow hunting rabbits. I know they were made of embroidery, because I touched them, but it must have been a very funny sort of embroidery, because the pictures were always changing. As long as you looked at them they stayed still, but if you looked away and back again they had altered. During dinner the builders had put a fresh storey on the house, the hunter had shot a bird with his cross-bow, and his dog had caught two rabbits.

The furniture was very funny, too. There was a bookcase made out of what looked like glass with the largest books in it that I ever saw, none of them less than a foot high, and bound in leather. There were cupboards running along the tops of the bookshelves. The chairs were beautifully carved, with high wooden backs, and there were two tables. One was made of copper, and had a huge crystal globe on it. The other was a solid lump of wood about ten feet long, four feet wide, and three feet high, with holes cut in it so that you could get your knees under it. There were various odd things hanging from the ceiling. At first I couldn't make out how the room was lit. Then I saw that the light came from plants of a sort I had never seen before, growing in pots. They had red, yellow and blue fruits about as big as tomatoes, which shone. They weren't disguised electric lamps, for I touched one and it was quite cold and soft like a fruit.

'Well,' said Mr Leakey, 'what would you like for dinner?'

'Oh, whatever you've got,' I said.

'You can have whatever you like,' he said. 'Please choose a soup.'

So I thought he probably got his dinner from a restaurant, and I said, 'I'll have Bortsch,' which is a red Russian soup with cream in it.

'Right,' he said, 'I'll get it ready. Look here, do you mind if we have dinner served the way mine usually is? You aren't easily frightened, are you?'

'Not very easily,' I said.

'All right, then, I'll call my servant, but I warn you he's rather odd.'

At that Mr Leakey flapped the tops and lobes of his ears against his head. It made a noise like when one claps one's hands, but not so loud. Out of a large copper pot about as big as the copper you wash clothes in, which was standing in one corner, came what at first I thought was a large wet snake. Then I saw it had suckers all down one side, and was really the arm of an octopus. This arm opened a cupboard and pulled out a large towel with which it wiped the next arm that came out. The dry arm then clung on to the wall with its suckers, and gradually the whole beast came out, dried itself, and crawled up the wall. It was the largest octopus I have ever seen; each arm was about eight feet long, and its body was as big as a sack. It crawled up the wall, and then along the ceiling, holding on by its suckers like a fly. When it got above the table it held on by one arm only, and with the other seven got plates and knives and forks out of the cupboards above the bookshelves and laid the table with them.

'That's my servant Oliver,' said Mr Leakey. 'He's much better than a person, because he has more arms to work with, and he can hold on to a plate with about ten suckers, so he never drops one.'

When Oliver the octopus had laid the table we sat down and he offered me a choice of water, lemonade, beer, and four different kinds of wine with his seven free arms, each of which held a different bottle. I chose some water and some very good red wine from Burgundy.

All this was so odd that I was not surprised to notice that my host was wearing a top hat, but I certainly did think it a little queer when he took it off and poured two platefuls of soup out of it.

'Ah, we want some cream,' he added. 'Come here, Phyllis.' At this a small green cow, about the size of a rabbit, ran out of a hutch, jumped on to the table, and stood in front of Mr Leakey, who milked her into a silver cream jug which Oliver had handed down for the purpose. The cream was excellent, and I enjoyed the soup very much.

'What would you like next?' said Mr Leakey.

'I leave it to you,' I answered.

'All right,' he said, 'we'll have grilled turbot, and turkey to follow. Catch us a turbot, please, Oliver, and be ready to grill it, Pompey.'

At this Oliver picked up a fishhook with the end of one of his arms and began making casts in the air like a fly-fisher. Meanwhile I heard a noise in the fireplace, and Pompey came out. He was a small dragon about a foot long, not counting

his tail, which measured another foot. He had been lying on the burning coals, and was red-hot. So I was glad to see that as soon as he got out of the fire he put a pair of asbestos boots which were lying in the fender on to his hind feet.

'Now, Pompey,' said Mr Leakey, 'hold your tail up properly. If you burn the carpet again, I'll pour a bucket of cold water over you. (Of course, I wouldn't really do that; it's very cruel to pour cold water on to a dragon, especially a little one with a thin skin),' he added in a low voice, which only I could hear. But poor Pompey took the threat quite seriously. He whimpered, and the yellow flames which were coming out of his nose turned a dull blue. He waddled along rather clumsily on his hind legs, holding up his tail and the front part of his body. I think the asbestos boots made walking rather difficult for him, though they saved the carpet, and no doubt kept his hind feet warm. But of course dragons generally walk on all four feet and seldom wear boots, so I was surprised that Pompey walked as well as he did.

I was so busy watching Pompey that I never saw how Oliver caught the turbot, and by the time I looked up at him again he had just finished cleaning it, and threw it down to Pompey. Pompey caught it in his front paws, which had cooled down a bit, and were just about the right temperature for grilling things. He had long thin fingers with claws on the end; and held the fish on each hand alternately, holding the other against his red-hot chest to warm it. By the time he had finished and put the grilled fish on to a plate which Oliver handed down Pompey was clearly feeling the cold, for his teeth were chattering, and he scampered back to the fire with evident joy.

'Yes,' said Mr Leakey, 'I know some people say it is cruel to let a young dragon cool down like that, and liable to give it a bad cold. But I say a dragon can't begin to learn too soon that life isn't all fire and flames, and the world is a colder place than he'd like it to be. And they don't get colds if you give them plenty of sulphur to eat. Of course a dragon with a cold is an awful nuisance to itself and everyone else. I've known one throw flames for a hundred yards when it sneezed. But that was a full-grown one, of course. It burned down one of the Emperor of China's palaces. Besides, I really couldn't afford to keep a dragon if I didn't make use of him. Last week, for example, I used his breath to burn the old paint off the door, and his tail makes quite a good soldering iron. Then he's really much more reliable than a dog for dealing with burglars. They might shoot a dog, but leaden bullets just melt the moment they touch Pompey. Anyway, I think dragons were meant for use, not ornament. Don't you?'

'Well, do you know,' I answered, 'I am ashamed to say that Pompey is the first live dragon I've ever seen.'

'Of course,' said Mr Leakey, 'how stupid of me. I have so few guests here except professional colleagues that I forgot you were a layman. By the way,' he went on, as he poured sauce out of his hat over the fish, 'I don't know if you've noticed anything queer about this dinner. Of course some people are more observant than others.'

'Well,' I answered, 'I've never seen anything like it before.'

For example at that moment I was admiring an enormous rainbow-coloured beetle which was crawling towards me over the table with a saltcellar strapped on its back.

'Ah well then,' said my host, 'perhaps you have guessed that I'm a magician. Pompey, of course, is a real dragon, but most of the other animals here were people before I made them what they are now. Take Oliver, for example. When he was a man he had his legs cut off by a railway train. I couldn't stick them on again because my magic doesn't work against machinery. Poor Oliver was bleeding to death, so I thought the only way to save his life was to turn him into some animal with no legs. Then he wouldn't have any legs to have been cut off. I turned him into a snail, and took him home in my pocket. But whenever I tried to turn him back into something more interesting, like a dog, it had no hind legs. But an octopus has really got no legs. Those eight ten-tacles grow out of its head. So when I turned him into an octopus, he was all right. And he had been a waiter when he was a man, so he soon learnt his job. I think he's much better than a maid because he can lift the plates from above, and doesn't stand behind one and breathe down one's neck. You may have the rest of the fish, Oliver, and a bottle of beer. I know that's what you like.'

Oliver seized the fish in one of his arms and put it into an

immense beak like a parrot's but much bigger, which lay in
the centre of the eight arms. Then he took a bottle of beer
out of a cupboard, unscrewed the cork with his beak, hoisted
himself up to the ceiling with two of his other arms, and
turned over so that his mouth was upwards. As he emptied
the bottle he winked one of his enormous eyes. Then I felt
sure he must be really a man, for I never saw an ordinary
octopus wink.

The turkey came in a more ordinary way. Oliver let down
a large hot plate, and then a dish cover on to it. There was
nothing in the cover, as I could see. Mr Leakey got up, took
a large wand out of the umbrella stand, pointed it at the dish
cover, said a few words, and there was the turkey steaming
hot when Oliver lifted the cover off it.

'Of course that's easy,' said Mr Leakey, 'any good conjuror
could do it, but you can never be sure the food you get in that
way is absolutely fresh. That's why I like to see my fish
caught. But birds are all the better for being a few days old.
Ah, we shall want some sausages too. That's easy.'

He took a small clay pipe out of his pocket and blew into
it. A large brown bubble came out of the other end, shaped
like a sausage. Oliver picked it off with the end of one of his
tentacles, and put it on a hot plate, and it was a sausage, because I ate it. He made six sausages in this way, and while I
was watching him Oliver had handed down the vegetables.
I don't know where he got them. The sauce and gravy came
out of Mr Leakey's hat, as usual.

Just after this the only accident of the evening happened.
The beetle who carried the salt-cellar round tripped over a
fold in the tablecloth and spilled the salt just in front of Mr
Leakey, who spoke to him very angrily.

'It's lucky for you, Leopold, that I'm a sensible man. If I
were superstitious, which I'm not, I should think I was going
to have bad luck. But it's you who are going to have bad
luck, if anyone. I've a good mind to turn you back into a man.

and if I do, I'll put you straight on to that carpet and send you to the nearest police station; and when the police ask you where you've been hiding, d'you think they'll believe you when you say you've been a beetle for the last year? Are you sorry?'

Leopold, with a great struggle, got out of his harness and rolled on to his back, feebly waving his legs in the air like a dog does when he's ashamed of himself.

'When Leopold was a man,' said Mr Leakey, 'he made money by swindling people. When the police found it out and were going to arrest him, he came to me for help, but I thought it served him right. So I said "If they catch you, you'll get sent to penal servitude for seven years. If you like I'll turn you into a beetle for five years, which isn't so long, and then, if you've been a good beetle, I'll make you into a man with a different sort of face, so the police won't know you." So now Leopold is a beetle. Well, I see he's sorry for spilling the salt. Now, Leopold, you must pick up all the salt you've spilt.'

He turned Leopold over on his front and I watched him begin to pick the salt up. It took him over an hour. First he picked it up a grain at a time in his mouth, lifted himself on his front legs, and dropped it into the saltcellar. Then he thought of a better plan. He was a beetle of the kind whose feelers are short and spread out into a fan. He started shovelling the salt with his feelers, and got on much quicker that way. But fairly soon he got uncomfortable. His feelers started to itch or something, and he had to wipe them with his legs. Finally he got a bit of paper and used it for a shovel, holding it with his front feet.

'That's very clever for a beetle,' said my host. 'When I turn him back into a man he'll be quite good with his hands, and I expect he'll be able to earn his living at an honest job.'

As we were finishing the turkey, Mr Leakey looked up anxiously from time to time.

'I hope Abdu'l Makkar won't be late with the straw-berries,' he said.

'Strawberries?' I asked in amazement, for it was the middle of January.

'Oh yes, I've sent Abdu'l Makkar, who is a jinn, to New Zealand for some. Of course it's summer there. He oughtn't to be long now, if he has been good, but you know what jinns are, they have their faults, like the rest of us. Curiosity, especially. When one sends them on long errands they will fly too high. They like to get up quite close to Heaven to overhear what the angels are saying, and then the angels throw shooting stars at them. Then they drop their parcels, or come home half scorched. He ought to be back soon, he's been away over an hour. Meanwhile we'll have some other fruit, in case he's late.'

He got up, and tapped the four corners of the table with his wand. At each corner the wood swelled; then it cracked, and a little green shoot came out and started growing. In a minute they were already about a foot high, with several leaves at the top, and the bottom quite woody. I could see from the leaves that one was a cherry, another a pear, and the third a peach, but I didn't know the fourth.

As Oliver was clearing away the remains of the turkey with four of his arms and helping himself to a sausage with a fifth, Abdu'l Makkar came in. He came feet first through the ceiling, which seemed to close behind him like water in the tank of the diving birds' house in the Zoo, when you look at it from underneath while a penguin dives in. It shook a little for a moment afterwards. He narrowly missed one of Oliver's arms, but alighted safely on the floor, bending his knees to break his fall, and bowing deeply to Mr Leakey. He had a brown face with rather a long nose, and looked quite like a man, except that he had a pair of leathery wings folded on his back, and his nails were of gold. He wore a turban and clothes of green silk.

'O peacock of the world and redresser of injustices,' he said, 'thy unworthy servant comes into the presence with rare and refreshing fruit.'

'The presence deigns to express gratification at the result of thy labours.'

'The joy of thy negligible slave is as the joy of King Solomon, son of David (on whom be peace, if he has not already obtained peace) when he first beheld Balkis, the queen of Sheba. May the Terminator of delights and Separator of companions be far from this dwelling.'

'May the Deluder of Intelligences never trouble the profundity of thine apprehension.'

'O dominator of demons and governor of goblins, what egregious enchanter or noble necromancer graces thy board?'

'It is written, O Abdu'l Makkar, in the book of the sayings of the prophet Shoaib, the apostle of the Midianites, that curiosity slew the cat of Pharaoh, king of Egypt.'

'That is a true word.'

'Thy departure is permitted. Awaken me at the accustomed hour. But stay! My safety razor hath no more blades and the shops of London are closed. Fly therefore to Montreal, where it is even now high noon, and purchase me a packet thereof.'

'I tremble and obey.'

'Why dost thou tremble, O audacious among the Ifreets?'

'O Emperor of enchantment, the lower air is full of aeroplanes, flying swifter than a magic carpet*, and each making a din like unto the bursting of the great dam of Sheba, and the upper air is infested with meteorites.'

'Fly therefore at a height of five miles and thou shalt avoid both the one peril and the other. And now, O performer of commands and executor of behests, thou hast my leave to depart.'

'May the wisdom of Plato, the longevity of Shiqq, the wealth of Solomon, and the success of Alexander, be thine.'

* This is of course a gross exaggeration.

'The like unto thee, with brazen knobs thereon.'

The jinn now vanished, this time through the floor. While he and Mr Leakey had been talking the trees had grown up to about four feet high, and flowered. The flowers were now falling off, and little green fruits were swelling.

'You have to talk like that to a jinn or you lose his respect. I hope you don't mind my not introducing you, but really jinns may be quite awkward at times,' said my host. 'Of course Abdu'l Makkar is a nice chap and means well, but he might be very embarrassing to you, as you don't know the Word of Power to send him away. For instance if you were playing cricket and went in against a fast bowler, he'd probably turn up and ask you "Shall I slay thine enemy, O Defender of the Stumps, or merely convert him into an he-goat of loathsome appearance and afflicted with the mange?" You know, I used to be very fond of watching cricket, but I can't do it now. Quite a little magic will upset a match. Last year I went to see the Australians playing against Gloucester, and just because I felt a little sympathetic with Gloucester-shire the Australian wickets went down like ninepins. If I hadn't left before the end they'd have been beaten. And after that I couldn't go to any of the test matches. After all, one wants the best side to win.'

We next ate the New Zealand strawberries, which were very good, with Phyllis's cream. While we did so Pompey, who acted as a sort of walking stove, came out again and melted some cheese to make a Welsh rarebit. After this we went on to dessert. The fruit was now quite ripe. The fourth tree bore half a dozen beautiful golden fruits shaped rather like apricots, but much bigger, and my host told me they were mangoes, which of course usually grow in India. In fact you can't make them grow in England except by magic. So I said I would try a mango.

'Aha,' said Mr Leakey, 'this is where I have a pull over Lord Melchett or the Duke of Westminster, or any other rich man. They might be able to get mangoes here by aero-plane, but they couldn't give them as dessert at a smart dinner-party.'

'Why not?' I asked.

'That shows you've never eaten one. The only proper place to eat a mango is in your bath. You see, it has a tough skin and a squashy inside, so when once you get through the skin all the juice squirts out. And that would make a nasty mess of people's white shirts. D'you ever wear a stiff-fronted shirt?'

'Not often.'

'A good thing too. You probably don't know why people wear them. It's a curious story. About a hundred years ago a great Mexican enchanter called Whiztopacoatl came over to Europe. And he got very annoyed with the rich men. He didn't so much mind their being rich, but he thought they spent their money on such ugly things, and were dreadfully stodgy and smug. So he decided to turn them all into turtles. Now to do that somebody has to say two different spells at the same time, which is pretty difficult, I can tell you. So Whiztopacoatl went round to an English sorcerer called Mr Benedict Barnacle, to borrow a two-headed parrot that be-longed to him. It was rather like one of those two-headed eagles they used to have on the Russian and Austrian flags. Then he was going to teach one of the heads one spell, and the other head the second spell; and when the parrot said both at once all the rich men would have turned into turtles. But Mr Barnacle persuaded him to be less fierce, so finally they agreed that for a hundred years the rich men in Europe should be made to wear clothes only fit for turtles. Because of course the front of a turtle is stiff and flat, and it is the only sort of animal that would be quite comfortable in a shirt with a stiff flat front. They made a spell to stiffen all the shirts, and of course it worked very well, but it's wearing off now, and soon nobody will wear such silly clothes any more.

'About your mango; you can eat it quite safely, if you just wait a moment while I enchant it so that it won't splash over you.'

Quite a short spell and a little wiggling of his wand were enough, and then I ate the mango. It was wonderful. It was the only fruit I have ever eaten that was better than the best strawberries. I can't describe the flavour, which is a mixture of all sorts of things, including a little resin, like the smell of a pine forest in summer. There is a huge flattish stone in the middle, too big to get into your mouth, and all round it a squashy yellow pulp. To test the spell I tried to spill some down my waistcoat, but it merely jumped up into my mouth. Mr Leakey ate a pear, and gave me the other five mangoes to take home. But I had to eat them in my bath because they weren't enchanted.

While we were having coffee (out of the hat, of course) Mr Leakey rubbed one corner of the table with his wand and it began to sprout with very fine green grass. When it was about as high as the grass on a lawn, he called Phyllis out of her hutch, and she ate some of it for her dinner. We talked for a while about magic, football, and the odder sorts of dog, such as Bedlington terriers and rough-haired Dachshunds, and then I said I must be getting home.

'I'll take you home,' said Mr Leakey, 'but when you have a day to spare you must come round and spend it with me, if you'd care to see the sort of things I generally do, and we might go over to India or Java or somewhere for the afternoon. Let me know when you're free. But now just stand on this carpet, and shut your eyes, because people often get giddy the first two or three times they travel by magic carpet.'

We got on to the carpet. I took a last look at the table, where Leopold had just finished picking up the salt, and was resting, while Phyllis was chewing the cud. Then I shut my eyes, my host told the carpet my address, flapped his ears, and I felt a rush of cold air on my cheeks, and a slight giddiness. Then the air was warm again. Mr Leakey told me to open my eyes, and I was in my sitting-room at home, five miles away. As the room is small, and there were a number of books and things on the floor, the carpet could not settle down properly, and stayed about a foot up in the air. Luckily it was quite stiff, so I stepped down off it, and turned the light on.

'Good-night,' said Mr Leakey, bending down to shake my hand, and then he flapped his ears and he and the carpet vanished. I was left in my room with nothing but a nice full feeling and a parcel of mangoes to persuade me that I had not been dreaming.

If you like this story I will tell you later on about a day I spent with Mr Leakey helping him with his work, and how Pompey was naughty and ran away down a volcano. But that is quite a different story. Still, I hope you think my friend Mr Leakey is a nice man. Because I do.

From *My Friend Mr Leakey* by J. B. S. Haldane (Cresset Press, London)

(See Note, page 217)

The White Cat

There was once a King who had three brave and handsome sons. He was growing old, yet he still enjoyed being a King and did not want to give up his throne. However, his subjects expected it of him, so he called his sons to him and said: 'I wish to give my crown to one of you, but it is only fair that you should consider *my* comfort and happiness first. I shall be lonely in the country when I retire, so I should like a pretty and intelligent little dog to keep me company. Which-ever of you brings me the best and smallest dog, shall be made King in my place.'

The Princes were exceedingly surprised to hear that their father wanted a little dog, but they promised that they would bring him the finest one they could find and return from their quest in a year's time. Each took a different road, agreeing to meet at the palace again after twelve months.

The youngest son was handsome, gay and courageous and had all the accomplishments a prince should have. He travelled through the world buying many dogs, but giving them all away again as not handsome or small enough to win a throne for him.

One night of thunder and rain, he lost his way in a forest. After riding through the darkness for a long time, he saw a glimmer of light and came to a magnificent palace. The gate was of gold covered with precious stones, and from it hung a kid's foot on a chain of diamonds. As soon as he pulled it, a bell rang and the gate opened. To his astonishment the Prince saw many hands holding torches and other hands pushed him gently forwards into a courtyard. Yet he saw no one—only the beckoning hands. Inside the palace a million lights were reflected from walls of crystal and mother-of-pearl. He passed through many beautiful rooms and in the sixty-first he saw a large armchair moving by itself towards a bright fire. The hands helped him to take off his wet clothes and gave him others of silk and gold to wear in their place.

Then the Prince was led into a fine hall where hung many paintings of the famous cats of history and fairy tale. An orchestra of cats was playing on guitars, mewing in different tones and scratching the strings with their claws.

Before the fire a table was laid for two and the Prince waited in some alarm to see who his host might be. As he watched, a little figure hidden in a long black veil, came softly in, preceded by two cats wearing cloaks and swords and followed by many cats in rich court dress.

The little figure approached and lifted its veil. The Prince saw a most beautiful little white cat, the most beautiful that ever was or ever will be. She had a most youthful and melancholy air and mewed so softly and sweetly that it went straight to his heart.

'Son of a King, you are welcome,' she said. 'My mewing Majesty is pleased to have such company.'

'Madame Cat,' replied the Prince bowing, 'it is generous of you to receive me with so much kindness. You are indeed a cat of rare distinction and I am honoured to meet you.'

The Cat and the Prince sat down and their supper was served by the hands. One dish was of pigeons, the other of mice. The little white Cat, seeing the Prince's hesitation, assured him that the dish of pigeons had been cooked especially for him and had no flavour of mice about it and, indeed, he found it delicious.

The Prince observed that the Cat was wearing a bracelet with a miniature set in diamonds on her paw. The portrait was so handsome and so like himself, that he exclaimed in astonishment. The little white Cat sighed so piteously as she saw his eyes upon the miniature, that he could not grieve her by asking whose the portrait was. Instead he talked gaily with his charming hostess and they afterwards watched a ballet danced by twelve cats and twelve monkeys.

The Prince slept pleasantly in a room hung about with tapestries of butterflies' wings in the shape and colours of a thousand different flowers. In the morning, the hands awakened him and dressed him in fine hunting clothes. In the courtyard more than five hundred cats were preparing for a hunt. The little white Cat was mounted on a spirited monkey and the Prince on a wooden horse which could gallop as swiftly as the wind. The cat hunters outran the rabbits and hares, while the kittens climbed the trees after birds.

So the days passed in entertainments of many kinds and the Prince forgot everything but his life with his dear little white Cat. A year went by so quickly that he could not believe it when the little Cat reminded him that it was time for him to return home.

'How can I find a dog small and handsome enough to win me a kingdom and a horse so swift that it can carry me home in three days!' exclaimed the Prince in dismay.

'Son of a King, I am your friend,' purred the little white Cat with much sweetness. 'The good wooden horse will carry you home as swiftly as need be. I have here a little dog that is more beautiful than the dog-star,' and, to the Prince's astonishment, she gave him an acorn.

'You are jesting!' he said. 'An acorn cannot contain a dog!'

'Put it to your ear,' said the white Cat. The Prince did so and heard quite plainly the bark of a tiny dog!

He thanked the little white Cat a thousand times and took a tender leave of her, promising to return as soon as he could. At the palace his brothers were surprised to see him ride into the courtyard on a *wooden* horse, and still more surprised when he showed them a miserable mongrel dog and pretended that this was his gift for his father. 'What a fool he is!' they thought. 'Well, one of us will win the throne if this is the best he can do.'

The two Princes had brought such dainty little dogs as their gift, that the King said he could not decide which he liked the better. While everyone was disputing about the matter, the youngest Prince took his acorn out of his pocket and opened it before the King. There lay a tiny dog, so pretty and nimble that the King could find nothing to say against it. It danced a *saraband* for him on its hind legs so well that he clapped his hands in admiration.

Nevertheless he was determined to keep his throne for another year, so he said that his sons must travel again and bring him a piece of cloth so fine that it would pass through the eye of a needle used for delicate embroidery.

The three brothers were angry, but what could they do? They set out once more on a quest.

The youngest Prince mounted his wooden horse and rode straight back to his little white Cat. She was lying in a basket lined with swansdown, looking sad and thin, but when she saw that the Prince had returned, she sprang up in delight. The Prince caressed her tenderly and she ordered that the palace should be lit by a thousand lamps in his honour. He told the little white Cat about his new quest, but she said that there were some cats in the palace who could spin exceedingly well and that she herself would watch over the work. All he had to do was to stay with her and enjoy himself—all would be well.

'If you love me, charming Pussy, tell me why it is that you can speak so perfectly and are so wise and sweet?' asked the Prince.

But the little white Cat would not answer him. 'Do not question me for I am not allowed to answer you,' she said. 'Remember that I shall always have a velvet paw for you.'

At the year's end she warned him that it was time for him to go. In the courtyard stood a fine carriage drawn by twelve snow-white horses. An escort of a thousand soldiers followed it and a hundred coaches carried many finely dressed noble-men. The little white Cat wished the Prince to travel home in state.

'But where is the material?' asked the Prince anxiously.

'Here is a walnut,' said the little white Cat. 'Crack it in your father's presence and inside you will find the cloth I promised you.'

'Thank you a thousand times, my dear little Cat,' cried the Prince. 'I do not really care whether I become a King or not—let me spend all my life with you instead.'

'You are kind to be fond of a little white Cat who, after all, is good for nothing but to catch mice,' said the little creature. 'You *must* go, for it is your destiny to become a King.'

The Prince kissed her soft paw and entered the carriage. At his father's palace, his two brothers were already show-ing the King pieces of cloth so delicate that they could pass through the eye of a darning needle. They hoped that their brother would not arrive at all.

Suddenly, with a loud flourish of trumpets and drums, the Prince drove up in his fine carriage with his thousand soldiers and the noblemen in their rich clothes.

He went immediately to the King and showed him the walnut the little white Cat had given him. While everyone watched, he cracked it open, expecting to see a piece of cloth inside it. Instead, there was a hazel nut. He cracked that—and inside was a cherry stone. He opened that—and inside there seemed to be only the kernel of the nut.

'Look at the fool!' cried his brothers. 'Does he think that a piece of cloth can be inside a nut so small!'

The Prince split the kernel—and inside was a grain of wheat. He cracked that—and inside was a millet seed. Now even his faith failed. 'Little white Cat, you have tricked me!' he thought sadly. Immediately he felt a cat's claw scratch him and saw a drop of blood start up upon his hand. Ashamed he opened the millet seed—and there was the piece of cloth. He drew it out, fold after fold, until it was five hundred yards in length. On it was woven in their natural colours beasts, birds and fishes; trees, plants and fruits; the sun, the moon and the stars of the sky. So delicate was the cloth that it passed easily through the eye of the finest needle that could be found.

The King and the two Princes looked on in silence. At last the King said grudgingly: 'This is indeed a marvel, but go and travel for yet another year. He who brings back the most beautiful maiden shall marry her and be crowned King in my place. I promise that this shall indeed be so.'

The youngest Prince knew that he had won both contests, thanks to his little white Cat, but he was too well bred to protest. He at once entered his carriage and drove back to his charming friend. As he approached the palace, he found the road strewn with flowers. The little white Cat was seated on a magnificent Persian carpet under a golden canopy. She received him with joy and soft mewings of pleasure.

'So, son of a King, you have returned once more without the crown,' she remarked. 'No matter, I will find you a beautiful maiden when it is time. Meanwhile, let us be merry and happy.'

So passed another year . . . Sometimes the Prince could not resist asking the little white Cat if she was a Fairy—or had she been enchanted into her present shape? But he could not persuade her to answer him.

Nothing goes faster than time passed without trouble or sorrow. At last the day came for the Prince to return to his father.

'You must take home a beautiful Princess,' said the white Cat, 'but first the time has come for you to release me from the spell that has turned me into a Cat. All you need to do is to cut off my head and my tail and fling them into the fire.'

'What!' cried the Prince in horror. 'How could I be so

cruel as to kill you! I could never so far forget my love for you!'

'Do as I bid you,' begged the little white Cat with tears in her eyes. 'It is the only way to save me.'

Then the Prince knew that it had to be done. He drew his sword and with a swift stroke cut off the white Cat's head and tail and threw them into the heart of the fire. Immediately the white Cat disappeared and in her place stood a most beautiful maiden. So beautiful was she that the Prince was unable to move or speak.

Into the room came a great company of lords and ladies, each carrying a cat's skin. They bowed to their Princess and withdrew. Taking the Prince's hand, she led him to a seat.

'Tell me your story,' begged the Prince.

'Think not that I have always been a cat,' she replied. 'My father was a King of six kingdoms, but the Fairies stole me when I was a child and shut me up in a high tower. There they planned to keep me until they married me to a horrible dwarf. But a King came to rescue me—he whose portrait I carry on my wrist—and we were to be married. Alas! the Fairies discovered our plans and the King was killed by a dragon. I, and all my lords and ladies, were transformed into cats. Only if I could find a Prince who was exactly like the King who should have married me, could I hope to be released from the spell. By your kindness to the little white Cat you know so well, you have given me back my rightful shape.'

'Come!' said the Prince eagerly. 'We will go to my father and our troubles will be at an end. My brothers cannot possibly have found a maiden more beautiful than you are!'

Together they stepped into a carriage even more magnificent than the one the little white Cat had ordered for the Prince. The horses were shod with emeralds and the nails in the shoes were diamonds. Such a thing has never been seen since! The Princess's mind was as matchless as her beauty and the young Prince was equally accomplished. As they rode, they talked about all the subjects that have ever been thought of.

When they were near the Prince's home, the Princess hid herself inside a crystal rock completely surrounded by silken curtains and carried by handsome young courtiers. The Prince remained in the carriage and admired the beautiful maidens his brothers had brought to court. When they asked him if he had found a bride, he smiled and said nothing.

The elder Princes rode in open carriages of gold and azure. Behind them came the youngest brother in a coach encrusted with diamonds. Behind him was carried the crystal rock at which everybody gazed in wonder. The two Princes ascended the Palace steps with their brides. The King received them graciously but said he was quite unable to decide which was the more beautiful. 'Have you no beautiful maiden?' he asked the youngest Prince.

'I have only a little white Cat,' replied the Prince. 'She mews so sweetly and has such velvet paws, that you will be delighted with her.'

'What, a *cat*!' cried the King and approached to open the crystal rock. Immediately the Princess, by means of magic, made it fly in pieces and stepped out unaided. She appeared like the sun from behind the clouds. Her fair golden hair fell in curls, she was crowned with flowers and her gown was of white lined with rose coloured taffeta. She made a deep curtsy to the King.

'Your Highness, I have not come to take away your throne,' she said. 'I have six kingdoms of my own. Allow me to offer one to you and one to each of your elder sons. Three will be enough for your youngest son and me, if you will allow him to be my husband.'

So, after a magnificent wedding, all the Princes became Kings and ruled over their kingdoms. They all lived happily ever after, but the youngest King and his Queen, who had once been a little white Cat, were the happiest of all.

Adapted by Eileen Colwell from the Countess D'Aulnoy's *Les Fées à la Mode*

(See Note, page 218)

The Ballad of Semmerwater

A North-country legend

Deep asleep, deep asleep,
Deep asleep it lies,
The still lake of Semmerwater
Under the still skies.

Many a fathom, many a fathom,
Many a fathom below,
In a king's tower and a queen's bower
The fishes come and go.

Once there stood by Semmerwater
A mickle town and tall;
King's tower and queen's bower,
And the wakeman on the wall.

Came a beggar halt and sore:
'I faint for lack of bread.'
King's tower and queen's bower
Cast him forth unfed.

He knocked at the door of the herdman's cot,
The herdman's cot in the dale.
They gave him of their oatcake,
They gave him of their ale.

He has cursed aloud that city proud,
He has cursed it in its pride;

He has cursed it into Semmerwater
Down the brant hillside;
He has cursed it into Semmerwater,
There to bide.

King's tower and queen's bower,
And a mickle town and tall;
By glimmer of scale and gleam of fin,
Folk have seen them all.

King's tower and queen's bower,
And weed and reed in the gloom;
And a lost city in Semmerwater,
Deep asleep till Doom.

From *The Poems of Sir William Watson 1878–1935* (Harrap, London)

(See Note, page 218)

The Little Pagan Faun

It was the eve of the second (or was it the third?) of all the Christmases when three little, rather self-esteeming, girl seraphs slipped out of the pearly gates of one of the heavenly spheres and ran merrily down the star-powdered stairways of the sky to sing carols to the Little Child. They were in fact the first of the waits, but they didn't know that they were.

When they got to the earth they found that they had made a slight miscalculation, and that they had still to go through a fir-wood before they came to the Babe's abode. Very beautiful the fir-wood looked in the frosty moonlight, and very beautiful the three little seraphs looked too as they hastened through it; while the faint and tender effulgence of their preparatory Paradise which was still about them made the pine-shadows deeper and more velvety and the three little seraphs themselves to look like three little glorified glow-worms.

Very lovely were their flower faces, you may be sure; and their best clothes, new on for the occasion, were all the scarlets, blues and golds that you can imagine. Their halcyon wings* too were folded closely about them and over their chests, for it was cold, and the snow and the moonlight were of course strange to them, and a little frightening besides, and so they ran tippity-tip-toe, each carrying her harp.

Now there sat in the wood on the stump of a tree a freckled little pagan faun; he was a very little one, and he was feeling uncommon lonesome, for his family had been a bit out of it for the last year or more; and so there he sat alone and occasionally he blew himself a few notes on his whistle for company, and between whiles he blew on his fingers to keep them warm.

Presently he saw the three little seraphs running tippity-tip-toe, and he thought that he'd never seen anything so lovely before, and he longed to be their playmate.

'Oh, you lovely little girl nymphs,' said he (for he knew no better), 'where are you going to?'

'Oh, you little pagan faun,' said the biggest one of the three little seraphs, 'we are going to sing carols to the Babe.'

'May I not come with you?' asked the little faun, ever so humbly; 'I can't sing carols, but I can play tunes on my whistle.'

'No, indeed, you little pagan faun,' replied the biggest one again, 'certainly *not*'; and her two little sparkly sisters said, '*What* an idea!' and then they all ran on, more tippity-tip-toe than ever, and came to the Babe's abode.

And then there they stood up, outside in the snow, and sang their carols more clearly and sweetly than thrushes.

And this is what they thought as they were singing:—

* Seraphs' wings, it has been stated, serve no practical purpose for flying with, their position on the shoulder being destructive to equilibrity if so used.

The first one thought, 'How beautifully I'm singing to-night, and how pleased the Babe will be to hear me!'

The second one thought, 'How sweetly I make my harp to ring, and how happy the Babe must be listening to it!'

The third one thought, 'How becoming to me are these beautiful clothes I have put on in the Babe's honour, and how he'll clap his hands to see me!'

Thus they thought as they sang together more clearly and sweetly than thrushes.

And in the sharp blue shadow of a pine-tree sat the little faun, who had followed them there, far off and unbeknownst, and his heart was in his little pagan throat, for never had he heard such tunes or seen such flower faces in all the forest.

And when the carols were sung the biggest little seraph went to the door and knocked, and the Lady of the House, who was the Babe's Mother, opened it and stood there hold-ing the Babe to her heart; and very sweet and kindly she looked with the firelight about her and her little son sitting grave and sleepily grey-eyed, in her arms.

And the three little seraphs all curtsied down to the snow, very low indeed, and then they all said together, 'We wish you a merry Christmas and we hope you liked our carols.'

Now as a matter of fact the Lady and the Babe hadn't heard the carols at all, not a note of 'em, though the singers had sung them more clearly and sweetly than thrushes; and this was, as the Lady knew at once and you will probably guess, because the three little self-esteeming seraphs had thought all the time only of their own sweet singing, their own sweet harping and their own lovely new clothes, and thus had rendered their music mute to those in whose honour it was intended.

But the Lady of the House was too kind and gentle to say this, for she hated to hurt anyone and the seraphs were really rather little darlings after all and meant very well. So she said:

'Thank you kindly, my dears'; and to her little son she said, 'Say "Thank you"', and the Babe said 'Thank you' (for he could just talk a little), speaking very clearly, gravely and politely.

And then she gave each of the three a bit of the Babe's birthday-cake, although it was a day too soon to cut it, and wished them a merry Christmas, and they ran off, tippity-tip-toe again, through the cold and the moonlit wood, their halcyon wings folded over their chests, until they came to the purple stairway, up which they ran, twinkling like stars, as fast as they'd run down it.

And when they'd gone and the house door was shut again, the little faun trotted timidly out of the shadows and began to blow a little tune on his whistle all about the summer and the hills of the sheep and the little woolly lambs; and as he played he thought to himself thus:—

'That was the most beautiful little boy shepherd I have ever seen, but he looks very grave, and I should love to make him laugh, so I will try very hard indeed to play my best for him, though he will think it very poor stuff after the carols.'

Now he hadn't played more than half his tune before the Lady came to the door of her own accord and said, 'Oh, you funny little faun, please to come in out of the cold and finish the pretty tune that you are so kindly playing to us in the kitchen, where we can hear it even better.'

So the faun stamped the snow off his hooves and came in and put his whistle to his lips and played his tune so merrily that the Babe laughed with delight, like robins singing; and the Lady laughed too, as gaily as a girl, tapping her foot the while in time with the music.

And when he'd done she gave the little faun an extra big bit of birthday-cake, and he asked, 'Please, my lady, mayn't I stay here for always and make tunes for the Babe to laugh at?'

And the Lady said very gently, 'No, my dear, that can't

be; you must go back to the wood and play your tunes to the rabbits and the shepherds and the shadows of the trees, and so help to make the world laugh and go round. But,' she added, 'you shall come and stay with the Babe and me when the world's gone round often enough; and a merry Christmas to you, my dear, and thank you.'

Now *you* mayn't be able to believe that the Lady promised the little pagan faun anything of the sort, but *I* can assure you that she did, and that he trotted off into the woods again, munching his cake and feeling much comforted about things, just as the clocks were striking twelve and it was Christmas Day.

From *The Little Pagan Faun and Other Fancies* by Patrick R. Chalmers (Jonathan Cape, London)

(See Note, page 219)

The Mousewife

Wherever there is an old house with wooden floors and
beams and rafters and wooden stairs and wainscots and skirt-
ing boards and larders, there are mice. They creep out on the
carpets for crumbs, they whisk in and out of their holes, they
run in the wainscot and between the ceiling and the floors.
There are no signposts because they know the way, and no
milestones because no one is there to see how they run.

In the old nursery rhyme, when the cat went to see the
queen, he caught a little mouse under her chair; that was
long long ago and that queen was different from our queen,
but the mouse was the same.

Mice have always been the same. There are no fashions in
mice, they do not change. If a mouse could have a portrait

painted of his great-great-grandfather, and his great-grand-father, it would be a portrait of a mouse to-day.

But once there was a little mousewife who was different from the rest.

She looked the same; she had the same ears and prick nose and whiskers and dewdrop eyes; the same little bones and grey fur; the same skinny paws and long skinny tail.

She did all the things a mousewife does: she made a nest for the mouse babies she hoped to have one day; she collected crumbs of food for her husband and herself; once she bit the tops off a whole bowl of crocuses; and she played with the other mice at midnight on the attic floor.

'What more do you want?' asked her husband.

She did not know what it was she wanted, but she wanted more.

The house where these mice lived belonged to a spinster lady called Miss Barbara Wilkinson. The mice thought the house was the whole world. The garden and the wood that lay round it were as far away to them as the stars are to you, but the mousewife used sometimes to creep up on the window sill and press her whiskers close against the pane.

In spring she saw snowdrops and appleblossom in the garden and bluebells in the wood; in summer there were roses; in autumn all the trees changed colour, and in winter they were bare until the snow came and they were white with snow.

The mousewife saw all these through the windowpane, but she did not know what they were.

She was a house mouse, not a garden mouse or a field mouse; she could not go outside.

'I think about cheese,' said her husband. 'Why don't you think about cheese?'

Then, at Christmas, he had an attack of indigestion through eating rich crumbs of Christmas cake. 'They have upset you,' said the mousewife. 'You must go to bed and be kept warm.' She decided to move the mousehole to a space behind the fender where it was warm. She lined the new hole with tufts of carpet wool and put her husband to bed wrapped in a pattern of grey flannel that Miss Wilkinson's lazy maid, Flora, had left in the dustpan. 'But I am grateful to Flora,' said the mousewife's husband as he settled himself comfortably in bed.

Now the mousewife had to find all the food for the family in addition to keeping the hole swept and clean.

She had no time for thinking.

While she was busy, a boy brought a dove to Miss Wilkinson. He had caught it in the wood. It was a pretty thing, a turtledove. Miss Wilkinson put it in a cage on the ledge of her sitting-room window.

The cage was an elegant one; it had gilt bars and a door that opened if its catch were pressed down; there were small gilt trays for water and peas. Miss Wilkinson hung up a lump of sugar and a piece of fat. 'There, you have everything you want,' said Miss Barbara Wilkinson.

For a day or two the dove pecked at the bars and opened and shut its wings. Sometimes it called 'Roo coo, roo coo'; then it was silent.

'Why won't it eat?' asked Miss Barbara Wilkinson. 'Those are the very best peas.'

A mouse family seldom has enough to eat. It is difficult to come by crumbs, especially in such a neat, tidy house as Miss Barbara Wilkinson's. It was the peas that first attracted the attention of the mousewife to the cage when at last she had time to go up on the window sill. 'I have been running here and there and everywhere to get us food,' she said, 'not allowing myself to come up on to the window sill, and here are these fine white peas, not to mention this piece of fat.' (She did not care for the sugar.)

She squeezed through the bars of the cage but, as she was taking the first pea from the tray, the dove moved its wings.

I cannot tell you how quickly the mousewife pressed herself
back through the bars and jumped down from the sill and
ran across the floor and whisked into her hole. It was
quicker than a cat can wink its eye. (She thought it was the
cat.)

In spite of her great fright she could not help thinking of
those peas. She was very hungry. 'I had better not go back,'
she said. 'There is something dangerous there,' but back she
went the very next day.

Soon the dove grew quite used to the mousewife going in
and out, and the mouse grew quite used to the dove.

'This is better,' said Miss Barbara Wilkinson. 'The dove
is eating its peas,' but, of course, he was not; it was the
mouse.

The dove kept his wings folded. The mousewife thought
him large and strange and ugly with the speckles on his
breast and his fine down. (She thought of it as fur, not
feathers.) He was not at all like a mouse; his voice was deep
and soft, quite unlike hers, which was a small, high squeaking. Most strange of all, to her, was that he let her take his
peas; when she offered them to him he turned his head aside
on his breast.

'Then at least take a little water,' begged the mousewife,
but he said he did not like water. 'Only dew, dew, dew,' he
said.

'What is dew?' asked the mousewife.

He could not tell her what dew was, but he told her how
it shines on the leaves and grass in the early morning for
doves to drink. That made him think of night in the woods
and of how he and his mate would come down with the first
light to walk on the wet earth and peck for food, and of how,
then, they would fly over the fields to other woods farther
away. He told this to the mousewife too.

'What is fly?' asked the ignorant little mousewife.

'Don't you know?' asked the dove in surprise. He stretched out his wings and they hit the cage bars. Still he struggled to spread them, but the bars were too close, and he sank back on his perch and sank his head on his breast.

The mousewife was strangely moved but she did not know why.

Because he would not eat his peas she brought him crumbs of bread and, once, a preserved blackberry that had fallen from a tart. (But he would not eat the blackberry.) Every day he talked to her about the world outside the window.

He told her of roofs and the tops of trees and of the rounded shapes of hills and the flat look of fields and of the mountains far away. 'But I have never flown as far as that,' he said, and he was quiet. He was thinking now he never would.

To cheer him the mousewife asked him to tell her about the wind; she heard it in the house on stormy nights, shaking the doors and windows with more noise than all the mice put together. The dove told her how it blew in the cornfields, making patterns in the corn, and of how it made different sounds in the different sorts of trees, and of how it blew up the clouds and sent them across the sky.

He told her these things as a dove would see them, as it flew, and the mousewife, who was used to creeping, felt her head growing as dizzy as if she were spinning on her tail, but all she said was, 'Tell me more.'

Each day the dove told her more. When she came he would lift his head and call to her, 'Roo coo, roo coo,' in his most gentle voice.

'Why do you spend so much time on the window sill?' asked her husband. 'I do not like it. The proper place for a mousewife is in her hole or coming out for crumbs and frolic with me.'

The mousewife did not answer. She looked far away.

Then, on a happy day, she had a nestful of baby mice. They were not as big as half your thumb, and they were pink and hairless, with pink shut eyes and little pink tails like threads. The mousewife loved them very much. The eldest, who was a girl, she called Flannelette, after the pattern of grey flannel. For several days she thought of nothing and no one else. She was also busy with her husband. His digestion was no better.

One afternoon he went over to the opposite wall to see a friend. He was well enough to do that, he said, but certainly not well enough to go out and look for crumbs. The mice-babies were asleep, the hole was quiet, and the mousewife began to think of the dove. Presently she tucked the nest up carefully and went up on the window sill to see him; also she was hungry and needed some peas.

What a state he was in! He was drooping and nearly ex-hausted because he had eaten scarcely anything while she had been away. He cowered over her with his wings and kissed her with his beak; she had not known his feathers were so soft or that his breast was so warm. 'I thought you had gone, gone, gone,' he said over and over again.

'Tut! Tut!' said the mousewife. 'A body has other things to do. I can't always be running off to you'; but, though she pretended to scold him, she had a tear at the end of her whisker for the poor dove. (Mouse tears look like millet seeds, which are the smallest seeds I know.)

She stayed a long time with the dove. When she went home, I am sorry to say, her husband bit her on the ear.

That night she lay awake thinking of the dove; mice stay up a great part of the night, but, towards dawn, they, too, curl into their beds and sleep. The mousewife could not sleep. She still thought of the dove. 'I cannot visit him as much as I could wish,' she said. 'There is my husband, and he has never bitten me before. There are the children, and it is surprising how quickly crumbs are eaten up. And no one would believe how dirty a hole can get if it is not attended to every day. But that is not the worst of it. The dove should

not be in that cage. It is thoughtless of Miss Barbara Wilkinson.' She grew angry as she thought of it. 'Not to be able to
scamper about the floor! Not to be able to run in and out, or
climb up the larder to get at the cheese! Not to flick in and
out and to whisk and to feel how you run in your tail! To sit
in the trap until your little bones are stiff and your whiskers
grow stupid because there is nothing for them to smell or
hear or see!' The mousewife could only think of it as a
mouse, but she could feel as the dove could feel.

Her husband and Flannelette and the other children were
breathing and squeaking happily in their sleep, but the
mousewife could hear her heart beating; the beats were
little, like the tick of a watch, but they felt loud and dis-
turbing to her. 'I cannot sleep,' said the mousewife, and then,
suddenly, she felt she must go then, that minute, to the dove.
'It is too late. He will be asleep,' she said, but still she felt
she should go.

She crept from her bed and out of the hole onto the floor
by the fender. It was bright moonlight, so bright that it made
her blink. It was bright as day, but a strange day, that made
her head swim and her tail tremble. Her whiskers quivered
this way and that, but there was no one and nothing to be
seen; no sound, no movement anywhere.

She crept across the pattern of the carpet, stopping here
and there on a rose or a leaf or on the scroll of the border. At
last she reached the wall and ran lightly up onto the window
sill and looked into the cage. In the moonlight she could see
the dove sleeping in his feathers, which were ruffled up so
that he looked plump and peaceful, but, as she watched, he
dreamed and called 'roo coo' in his sleep and shivered as if
he moved. 'He is dreaming of scampering and running free,'
said the mousewife. 'Poor thing! Poor dove!'

She looked out into the garden. It too was as bright as day,
but the same strange day. She could see the tops of the trees
in the wood, and she knew, all at once, that was where the

dove should be, in the trees and the garden and the wood.

He called 'roo coo' again in his sleep—and she saw that the window was open.

Her whiskers grew still and then they stiffened. She thought of the catch on the cage door. If the catch were pressed down, the door opened.

'I shall open it,' said the mousewife. 'I shall jump on it and hang from it and swing from it, and it will be pressed down; the door will open and the dove can come out. He can whisk quite out of sight. Miss Barbara Wilkinson will not be able to catch him.'

She jumped at the cage and caught the catch in her strong little teeth and swung. The door sprang open, waking the dove.

He was startled and lifted his wings and they hit hard against the cage so that it shivered and the mousewife was almost shaken off.

'Hurry! Hurry!' she said through her teeth. In a heavy sidelong way he sidled to the door and stood there looking. The mousewife would have given him a push, but she was holding down the catch.

At the door of the cage the dove stretched his neck towards the open window. 'Why does he not hurry?' thought the mousewife. 'I cannot stay here much longer. My teeth are cracking.'

He did not see her or look towards her, then—clap—he took her breath away so that she fell. He had opened his wings and flown straight out. For a moment he dipped as if he would fall, his wings were cramped, and then he moved them and lifted up and up and flew away across the tops of the trees.

The mousewife picked herself up and shook out her bones and her fur.

'So that is to fly,' she said. 'Now there is no one to tell me about the hills and the corn and the clouds. I shall forget them. How shall I remember when there is no one to tell me and there are so many children and crumbs and bits of fluff to think of?' She had millet tears, not on her whiskers but in her eyes.

'Tut! tut!' said the mousewife and blinked them away. She looked out again and saw the stars.

It has been given to few mice to see the stars; so rare is it that the mousewife had not even heard of them, and when she saw them shining she thought at first they must be new brass buttons. Then she saw they were very far off, farther than the garden or the wood, beyond the farthest trees. 'But not too far for me to see,' she said. She knew now that they were not buttons but something far and big and strange. 'But not so strange to me,' she said, 'for I have seen them. And I have seen them for myself,' said the mousewife, 'without the dove. I can see for myself,' said the mousewife, and slowly, proudly, she walked back to bed.

She was back in the hole before her husband waked up, and he did not know that she had been away.

Miss Barbara Wilkinson was astonished to find the cage empty next morning and the dove gone. 'Who could have let it out?' asked Miss Wilkinson. She suspected Flora and never knew that she was looking at someone too large and that it was a very small person indeed.

The mousewife is a very old lady mouse now. Her whiskers are grey and she cannot scamper any more; even her running is slow. But her great-great-grandchildren, the children of the children of the children of Flannelette and Flannelette's brothers and sisters, treat her with the utmost respect.

She is a little different from them, though she looks the same. I think she knows something they do not.

The Mousewife by Rumer Godden (Macmillan, London, and Viking, N.Y.)

(See Note, page 220)

The Hurdy-Gurdy Man

It was on a bright spring morning that the hurdy-gurdy man came to town. The sky was blue; there were little green leaves on the elms, and the sun shone down on the roofs and pavements, making everything look clean and newly-washed. The shopkeepers were just taking down their shutters and the housewives shaking rugs, and there was a pleasant early morning smell of breakfasts cooking, which made the hurdy-gurdy man feel very hungry, for he had walked a long way since daybreak. And the first person he set eyes on, as he strode whistling into the town with his hurdy-gurdy strapped to his back, was the fat woman in the Ham and Beef Shop, just sweeping her doorstep.

'Good morning! Can I get a cup of tea here?' asked the hurdy-gurdy man.

The fat woman looked him up and down, for he was very shabby. Still, a customer was a customer, and she was just about to say 'yes', when she caught sight of a queer little wrinkled face staring at her over his shoulder. It belonged to the hurdy-gurdy man's monkey, who was perched up there on top of the organ, making no sound but just gazing at her out of his dark solemn eyes.

'You may buy a cup of tea,' she said, 'but you can't bring that nasty grinning monkey into my shop, for monkeys I can't and won't abide!'

'Then, in that case,' said the hurdy-gurdy man politely, 'we will do without the tea!'

And off he strolled up the street with his monkey on his shoulder.

Presently he came to the Bakery, and there was the Baker

in his shirt-sleeves, setting out his fresh loaves on the counter.

'Good morning! Can I get a cup of tea here and a loaf of bread?' asked the hurdy-gurdy man.

But the Baker, too, had caught sight of the monkey, staring at him with unwinking eyes.

'I can sell you bread,' he answered, 'but you'll get your tea somewhere else, for I won't have that foreign-looking beast sitting at my table and scaring my customers.'

'Then we won't have the bread either,' said the hurdy-gurdy man, and he went on his way.

Now it so happened that the hurdy-gurdy man had come to the worst little town he could possibly have found. It was a neat and prosperous little town, but all the people who lived in it were so busy being neat and prosperous that they had no time for anything else. Everyone went about his or her business all day long just as serious as ants in an ant-hill. The housewives worked from morning till night. Every windowpane was polished till it shone; every hedge was clipped, and on the front lawns there wasn't so much as a single grass-blade out of place. And as for such things as trams or stray dogs or organ-grinders, the little town would have none of them.

As the hurdy-gurdy man strolled on up the street that spring morning he looked about him. He noticed the shiny windowpanes and the front curtains all starched and stiff, and the neat lawns, and once in a while he frowned, and once in a while he nodded, and once in a while he reached his hand up to scratch the ear of the little monkey who sat so quietly on his shoulder. And so he went his way, whistling through his teeth, and presently he reached the end of the Green, where the tall elm trees stood. And there, a little back from the road, he came upon two small cottages, side by side.

These two little cottages didn't look as if they belonged to the town at all, and that was exactly what the town itself felt about them. They were shabby and tumble-down; their walls needed painting and their front fences were unmended, and their front gardens, instead of being neat and tidy like all the other front gardens round about, were just a tangle of roses and lilacs and syringa bushes, growing just as they pleased. And in one yard there were yellow day-lilies crowding against the palings and overflowing into the street itself, and in the other a great bed of marigolds, hollowed out in the middle, where a big striped cat lay curled up asleep in the sun.

Most unsightly little cottages, the whole town agreed.

But for all that there was something gay and cheerful about them, if only for the way the lilacs nodded in the breeze, and the sturdy look of the geraniums on the window-sills. And there was something cheerful about the people who lived in them, which was more than could be said for the rest of the townspeople, and more, too, than those same townspeople could understand.

For why should Mrs Meeks be cheerful, with a seven-year-old boy called Tommy to cook and wash and buy shoes for, and only an odd day's work to be had now and then at scrubbing or spring-cleaning? While as for Miss Gay, the Dressmaker next door, everyone knew she was as poor as a church mouse, and wouldn't be able to live at all if the neighbours didn't kindly give her a few curtains to hem once in a while, because, after all, she did sew more cheaply than anyone else.

None of these things the hurdy-gurdy man knew, but something about the cottages seemed to please him, for he walked right in through the first gateway—which happened to be Miss Gay's—and up the little path past the marigolds and the sleeping cat, and was just about to knock at the door, when the door opened, and there stood Miss Gay herself, a little flustered, and peering short-sightedly through her glasses.

Straight past him she peered, and straight at the little

brown face staring over his shoulder, and the first thing she
said was:

'Why, look at the dear little monkey!'

At that the monkey moved for the first time. He scrambled
down from his master's shoulder and ran through the doorway into Miss Gay's kitchen. He climbed into a chair at the
table where Miss Gay had been eating her breakfast, and
there he sat.

'See that, bless him!' Miss Gay exclaimed. 'He must be
hungry! And perhaps you'd take a cup of tea, too,' she added,
turning to the hurdy-gurdy man. 'It's early in the day to be
travelling.'

'I will indeed, thank you,' said the hurdy-gurdy man, and
he followed her in and sat down at the table and took the
monkey on his knee.

Miss Gay asked him no questions, but she bustled about
and fetched tea and bread and home-made jam, and an apple
for the monkey. When everything was on the table, she said:

'And now, if you'll excuse me, I must go and call Tommy
Meeks, next door, for he'd never forgive me if he knew I'd
had a monkey to breakfast, and he wasn't here to see him.'

And she fluttered out at the door calling: 'Tommy! Tommy
Meeks! Come and see who's here!'

Tommy was tanned and brown-haired and freckled, and
his toes, as usual, were nearly out of his shoes, but the
monkey took to him amazingly, and he to the monkey. And
while they were making friends, and the monkey offering
Tommy bites of his apple, the hurdy-gurdy man asked Miss
Gay what she thought about the town.

'They're nice people,' Miss Gay told him. 'No one could
say they aren't kind. But there—they're just taken up with
their own affairs. Now, where I was born the folk were all
neighbourly, and they liked to joke or gossip, and if there
was music, they'd gather round from miles to hear it! But
here they aren't like that. They're folk that like everything

quiet. And as for a bit of music, you couldn't get them to listen to it!'

'They'll listen to my music,' said the hurdy-gurdy man.

'Goodness knows they need it,' Miss Gay nodded. 'Though I shouldn't be talking about my neighbours this way. But I always liked to see things cheerful!'

'How many tunes can your organ play?' interrupted Tommy. He wanted to know all about it, and how the stops worked.

'It can play three tunes, but as a rule there are only two of them I ever need to play,' said the hurdy-gurdy man. 'If I pull out that third stop there, then it plays the third tune.'

'And what is that like?' Tommy asked.

'It's a queer sort of a tune,' said the hurdy-gurdy man, 'and I don't play it so often.'

'Oh, I hope you play it to-day!' Tommy cried.

'That we'll see about,' said the hurdy-gurdy man. 'And now, thank you very much for the breakfast, and we'll have to be getting along!'

At that the monkey swallowed his last bite of apple, very quickly, and jumped to his master's shoulder, and the man picked up his hurdy-gurdy once more and set out.

Tommy went with him. He was very anxious to hear the music, and he didn't mean to lose sight of his friend the monkey.

When they came to the middle of the Green the hurdy-gurdy man stopped. He unslung the strap from his shoulder and began to play. As he turned the handle the first little tune tinkled out, a funny wheezy old tune, such as all hurdy-gurdies play, with a lot of squeaks and trills and deep rumblings to it.

No one seemed to be listening. Here and there a window blind was whisked aside and then whisked back again, in an annoyed sort of way. But no one paid any real attention.

But by the time he had begun his little tune for the second time, someone had heard him certainly.

The children had heard him.

For it is a queer thing that, whatever the grown people may be like in a town, the children are the same the world

over, and all children love a hurdy-gurdy. So out they came trooping, to gather round the hurdy-gurdy man and his monkey. Children just escaped from the breakfast table, boys and girls on their way to school, they all came scampering across the grass, shouting one to another and paying no heed at all to their parents, who scolded them from the doorways.

All they thought of was to see the monkey and listen to the hurdy-gurdy.

When the hurdy-gurdy man played his second tune it was even better than the first. It went faster and had a gayer lilt to it, so that all the children began to prance and jump, while the monkey pulled his cap off and bobbed and ducked to them till they yelled with joy.

And now the school bell began to ring. 'Ding-dong, ding-dong,' it went, but no one paid any attention to it. And after it had been ringing for a long time, and still no one obeyed it, the Teacher herself came out on the school-house steps, and began to clap her hands at the children very sternly and angrily.

But no one paid any attention to her, either.

Every child in the town, by now, was gathered round the hurdy-gurdy.

Such a thing had never been heard of before!

The fathers and mothers were furious, the School Teacher was furious. The Town Clerk was the most furious of all, for he liked quiet and order, and here, almost under the very Town Hall windows, was such a hullabaloo as he had never heard before. He wanted to fetch the police, but he knew that the town Policeman (there was only one) was in bed that day with a bad cold in his head, and couldn't be routed out. For when had their quiet orderly town ever expected to *need* a policeman?

Out came the Town Clerk himself, waving his hands and spluttering, his pen behind his ear.

'You must go away,' he cried. 'This is disgraceful! Street music isn't allowed in this town!'

But the hurdy-gurdy man went right on grinding out his tune.

'Do you hear me?' shouted the Town Clerk. 'And as for you,' he went on, glaring at the mob of children, 'go right into school this minute, every one of you!'

But through the noise of the hurdy-gurdy his words only sounded like 'Hoo—hoo—hoo!'

'Hoo—hoo!' the children shouted back at him, for they were feeling too happy and excited by this time to care what anyone said to them, whether they could hear it or not.

'I shall fetch the Mayor!' stormed the Town Clerk.

And fetch the Mayor he did.

The Mayor came, puffing and blowing, with his hat on the back of his head. He had been an auctioneer before he was made Mayor, and he still had the auctioneer's manner.

'Now then,' boomed the Mayor. 'Now then!'

It sounded like: 'Step up! Step up!'

And everyone stepped up, for by this time half the towns-people had gathered round, too.

The Mayor pulled a copy of the town by-laws from his pocket and began to read, very fast.

'Whereas, it is hereby decreed that any person or persons causing an obstruction—'

He had just got to the word 'obstruction' when the monkey jumped down from the hurdy-gurdy man's shoulder, took a flying leap on to the Mayor's broad back, snatched the copy of the by-laws out of his hand and scrambled up with it to the top of the village flagstaff, where he sat, tearing the paper into tiny shreds and dropping them down on the heads of the crowd below.

'Arrest that monkey!' shouted the Mayor. 'Shoot that monkey!'

'Don't you dare!' piped a thin little voice from the out-skirts of the crowd. It belonged to Miss Gay, the Dress-maker.

'Shoot him!' shouted the townspeople. 'Shoot him!'

There was a great confusion and noise and fuss, with everyone yelling at the tops of their voices but, through it all, the hurdy-gurdy kept on its tinkling tune.

Meantime Tommy Meeks, who was far more interested in

the hurdy-gurdy than in anything else, tugged suddenly at the organ-man's sleeve.

'Play the third tune!' he said. 'I want to hear the third tune!'

The hurdy-gurdy man looked down at Tommy, and he looked round on the crowd.

'Yes,' he said, 'I think now we'll play the third tune!'

And he pushed in that little stop at the side of the hurdy-gurdy that Tommy had been so anxious about all the time.

All at once the hurdy-gurdy broke out into the very maddest and jiggiest little tune that has ever been heard. It was like all the tunes in the world rolled up into one, and yet it was like none of them. It was the sort of little tune that set your brain whirling and your feet jigging, whether you wanted or not.

At the first notes the townspeople forgot all about the monkey and the Mayor and the flagstaff. They just stood there and stared. And then a very queer and surprised look came over all their faces. And their heads began to nod and their feet began to fidget, and before they knew it they were all dancing!

There they all were, the Town Clerk and the Chemist, the Grocer and the cross Baker, the fat woman from the Ham and Beef Shop, the housewives and all the rest of them, dancing away to the music of the hurdy-gurdy; cheery Mrs Meeks having the time of her life for once, and little Miss Gay holding up her skirts and skipping with the best of them!

'Stop it!' gasped the Mayor. 'Stop it, stop it!' begged the School Teacher, her head bobbing and her spectacles bouncing on her nose. But no one could stop it, and soon they were too much out of breath even to gasp.

Round and round the Green they went, children and grown folk all together, dancing away like mad, while the hurdy-gurdy wheezed out its strange jiggety tune, and the monkey, who by now had slid down the flagstaff again and was perched on his master's shoulder, waved his little red cap and cheered them on.

And then, suddenly, the music stopped.

Down everyone tumbled, one on top of another, too dizzy to stand on their feet another second. The Town Clerk went sprawling on the grass; the Ham and Beef Shop lady clutched the Baker, and over they went in a heap, and the School Teacher sat down plump on the Mayor's lap. Red-faced, panting and out of breath, there they sat and stared at one another.

And very silly they all felt!

There was only one thing to do about it. Everyone began to laugh. The others all looked so foolish that they couldn't help it. They laughed and they choked, and they held their sides and laughed again.

The Mayor was the first who could get his breath to speak. And what he said was the strangest thing of all. He said:

'Let's have a picnic!'

For that's what the music had done to *him*!

'A picnic, a picnic!' shouted all the children. 'A picnic!' shouted everyone else.

The Ham and Beef Shop lady billowed to her feet.

'I'll bring some hot dogs and sandwiches!' she cried.

'I'll bring the buns!' cried the Baker.

'I'll fetch the ice cream and the ginger beer!' shouted the man from the Sweet Shop.

And away they went.

It was the best picnic the town had ever had. In fact, it was the very first picnic that the town had ever had. No one worried about anything. There was no time to run home and brush one's hair or put on one's best clothes. Everyone just sat round on the grass in a big circle, with the Mayor in the middle, and ate and drank and enjoyed themselves.

And it was not until Tommy Meeks was munching his

seventh doughnut and scraping his third plate of ice cream, that he looked around and cried out suddenly: 'Why, where is the hurdy-gurdy man?'

Where, indeed?

The hurdy-gurdy man had vanished. No one had seen him go. He had just disappeared.

Somewhere undoubtedly, at that monent, he was walking the road whistling, with his monkey on his shoulder, looking for another little town that might need his music.

The Hurdy-Gurdy Man by Margery Williams Bianco (Walck, N.Y.)

(See Note, page 220)

Lazy Tok

'Have you ever heard the story of Lazy Tok?' drawled the Slow Loris when the animals met at the drinking pool in the evening.

'We never have,' cried all the animals at once.

'Very well,' said the Slow Loris, 'if you're very quiet and don't scuffle and stamp I'll tell you.'

Tok was born lazy, began the Slow Loris, clearing his throat. When she was a baby everybody said what a good baby she was because she never cried, but really she was too lazy to cry. It was too much trouble. The older she grew the lazier she became, until she got so lazy that she was too tired to go and look for food for herself. One day she was sitting by the side of the river, too lazy to wonder where her next meal was coming from, when a Nipah tree on the other side of the river spoke to her.

'Good evening, Tok,' he said. 'Would you like to know how to get your meals without having to work for them?'

Tok was too lazy to answer, but she nodded her head.

'Well, come over here and I'll tell you,' said the Nipah tree.

'Oh, I'm much too weary to come over there. Couldn't you come over here?' yawned Tok.

'Very well,' said the Nipah tree, and he bent over the river.

'Just tear off one of my branches,' he said.

'Oh, what a nuisance,' said Tok. 'Couldn't you shake one down yourself?'

So the Nipah tree shook himself and down dropped one of his branches at Tok's feet.

'Good evening, Tok,' said the Nipah branch. 'Would you like to be able to get your meals without having to work for them?'

Tok was too lazy to answer, but she nodded her head.

'Well,' said the Nipah branch, 'all you've got to do is to make a basket out of me.'

'Good gracious,' said Tok. 'What a bother. Couldn't you make yourself into a basket without my help?'

'Oh, very well,' said the Nipah branch, and he made him-self into a nice, neat, wide, fat basket.

'Good evening, Tok,' said the Basket. 'Would you like to be able to get your meals without having to work for them?'

Tok was too lazy to answer, but she nodded her head.

'Then pick me up,' said the Basket, 'and carry me to the edge of the road and leave me there.'

'Good gracious me,' said Tok, 'do you think I'm a slave? Couldn't you pick yourself up and go without bothering me?'

'Oh, very well,' said the Basket, and he picked himself up and went off and laid himself down by the side of the road.

He hadn't been waiting there long before a fat Chinaman came along.

'Shen mao tung shi!' said the Chinaman. 'Here's a fine basket that somebody has dropped. It will just do for me to carry my goods home from market in.'

So he picked up the Basket and went off to market with it. He soon had it full of rice, potatoes, pumeloes, durians, dried shrimps, and other things too numerous to mention, and when it was full up he started off home with it.

After a while he felt hot and tired, so he put the Basket down under a tree and went off to sleep. As soon as the Basket saw that the Chinaman was fast asleep up it jumped, and ran away back to Lazy Tok.

'Here I am,' said the Basket. 'Here I am, full to the brim. You have only to empty me out, and you will have enough food to last you for a week.'

'Dear, oh, dear!' said Lazy Tok. 'What a bother. Couldn't you empty yourself out?'

'Oh, very well,' said the Basket cheerfully, and he emptied himself into Tok's lap.

Next week, when Tok had eaten all the food, the Basket went off again and lay down on the grass by the side of the road. This time a Booloodoopy came along, and when he saw the Basket he thought it would be fine to carry his goods home from market; so he picked it up and took it off to the market. When it was full of pineapples and pumeloes and all sorts of nice things too numerous to mention, he started off home with it, but he hadn't gone far before he felt tired and hot and sat down on the side of the road to have a nap. As soon as he had fallen asleep up jumped the Basket and ran home to Lazy Tok.

So every week the Basket got itself carried to the market and came back full of fruit and rice and all sorts of other nice

things too numerous to mention; and Lazy Tok sat on the
river bank and ate and ate and ate and got fatter and fatter
and lazier and lazier, until she became so fat and so lazy that
she simply couldn't feed herself.

'Here we are waiting to be eaten,' said the fruit and the
shrimps and the other nice things one day.

'Oh, bother,' said Lazy Tok. 'Couldn't you feed me yourself, without giving me so much trouble?'

'We'll try,' said the fruit and the shrimps and the other
nice things; so after that they used to drop into her mouth
without giving her any unnecessary trouble.

So Lazy Tok grew fatter and FATTER and F A T T E R
and lazier and LAZIER and L A Z I E R; until one day the
Basket went off to lie down by the side of the road, just when
the fat Chinaman who had picked it up the first time came
along.

'Twee!' he said angrily. 'There you are, you thieving
scoundrel!' and he picked up the Basket and took it to the
market to show all his friends what had been robbing them.
All his friends came round and looked at the Basket and cried,
'That is the rascal that has been robbing us!'

So they took the Basket and filled it full of soldier ants,
lizards, hot-footed scorpions, bees, wasps, leeches, and all
sorts of other creeping, prickling, biting, stinging, tickling,
and itchy things far too unpleasant to mention; after which
they let the Basket go.

Off ran the Basket with his load of bugs and beetles and
centipedes and gnats and ran straight home to Lazy Tok.

'What have you got for me to-day?' asked Lazy Tok.

'You'd better get up and look,' said the Basket.

'Oh, dear me, no!' said Tok. 'I'm so tired, and I feel I
couldn't stir a finger. Just empty yourself into my lap.'

So the Basket emptied the ants and beetles, and other things
too horrible to mention, into Lazy Tok's lap.

Lazy Tok got up and ran and ran and ran, as she had

never run in her life before. But the ants, beetles, and scorpions ran after her, and the leeches and lizards crawled after her, and the wasps and bees flew after her; and they stung her and bit her and pricked her; and the harder she ran the harder they bit her. As far as I know she may be running still, and she is thinner than ever.

From *The Meeting Pool* by Mervyn Skipper (Angus and Robertson, London)

(See Note, page 221)

The Nightingale

In China, you must know, the Emperor is a Chinaman, and all those around him are Chinamen, too. It is many years since all this happened, and for that very reason it is worth hearing, before it is forgotten.

The Emperor's palace was the most beautiful in the world; built all of fine porcelain and very costly, but so fragile that it was very difficult to touch, and you had to be very careful in doing so. The most wonderful flowers were to be seen in the garden, and to the most beautiful flowers, silver bells, tinkling bells were tied, for fear people should pass by without noticing them. How well everything had been thought out in the Emperor's garden! This was so big, that the gardener himself did not know where it ended. If you walked on and on you came to the most beautiful forest, with tall trees and big lakes. The wood stretched right down to the sea which was blue and deep; great ships could pass underneath the branches, and here a nightingale had made its home, and its singing was so entrancing that the poor fisherman, though he had so many other things to do, would lie still and listen when he was out at night drawing in his nets.

174

'How beautiful it is!' he said; but then he was forced to think about his own affairs, and the Nightingale was for-gotten. The next day, when it sang again, the fisherman said the same thing: 'How beautiful it is!'

Travellers from all the countries of the world came to the Emperor's town, and expressed their admiration of the palace and the garden, but when they heard the Nightingale, they all said: 'This is the best of all!'

Now, when these travellers came home, they told of what they had seen. And scholars wrote many books about the town, the palace and the garden, but nobody left out the Nightingale; it was always spoken of as the most wonderful of all they had seen. And those who had the gift of the Poet, wrote the most delightful poems all about the Nightingale in the wood near the deep lake.

The books went round the world, and in the course of time some of them reached the Emperor. He sat in his golden chair, and read and read, nodding his head every minute; for it pleased him to read the beautiful descriptions of the town, the palace and the garden.

'But the Nightingale is the best of all,' he read.

'What is this?' said the Emperor. 'The Nightingale! I know nothing whatever about it. To think of there being such a bird in my Kingdom—nay, in my very garden—and I have never heard it. And to think one should learn such a thing for the first time from a book!'

Then he summoned his Lord-in-Waiting, who was such a grand personage that if anyone inferior in rank ventured to speak to him, or ask him about anything, he merely answered 'P' which meant nothing whatever.

'There is said to be a most wonderful bird, called the Nightingale,' said the Emperor; 'they say it is the best thing in my great Kingdom. Why have I been told nothing about it?'

'I have never heard it mentioned before,' said the Lord-in-Waiting. 'It has certainly never been presented at court.'

'It is my good pleasure that it shall appear to-night and sing before me!' said the Emperor. 'The whole world knows what is mine, and I myself do not know it.'

'I have never heard it mentioned before,' said the Lord-in-Waiting. 'I will seek it, and I shall find it.'

But where was it to be found? The Lord-in-Waiting ran up and down all the stairs, through the halls and passages, but not one of all those whom he met had ever heard a word about the Nightingale; so the Lord-in-Waiting ran back to the Emperor and told him that it must certainly be a fable invented by writers of books.

'Your Majesty must not believe all that is written in books. It is pure invention, something which is called the Black Art.'

'But,' said the Emperor, 'the book in which I have read this was sent to me by His Majesty, the Emperor of Japan, and therefore this cannot be a falsehood. I *will* hear the Nightingale. It must appear this evening! It has my Imperial favour, and if it fails to appear the Court shall be trampled upon after the Court has supped.'

'Tsing-pe!' said the Lord-in-Waiting, and again he ran up and down all the stairs, through all the halls and passages, and half the Court ran with him, for they had no wish to be trampled upon. And many questions were asked about the wonderful Nightingale, of whom all had heard except those who lived at Court.

At last, they met a poor little girl in the kitchen. She said: 'Oh, yes! The Nightingale! I know it well. How it can sing! Every evening I have permission to take the broken pieces from the table to my poor sick mother who lives near the sea-shore, and on my way back, when I feel tired, and rest a while in the wood, then I hear the Nightingale sing, and my eyes are filled with tears; it is as if my mother kissed me.'

'Little kitchen-maid,' said the Lord-in-Waiting, 'I will get a permanent place for you in the Court Kitchen and permission to see the Emperor dine, if you can lead us to the Nightingale; for it has been commanded to appear at Court to-night.'

So they started off all together where the bird used to sing; half the Court went, too. They were going along at a good pace, when suddenly they heard a cow lowing.

'Oh,' said a Court-Page. 'There it is! What wonderful power for so small a creature! I have certainly heard it before.'

'No, those are the cows lowing,' said the little kitchen-maid. 'We are a long way from the place yet.'

Then the frogs began to croak in the marsh. 'Glorious,' said the Court-Preacher. 'Now, I hear it—it is just like little church-bells.'

'No, those are the frogs,' said the little kitchen-maid. 'But now I think we shall soon hear it.'

And then the Nightingale began to sing.

'There it is,' said the little girl. 'Listen, listen—there it sits!' And she pointed to a little grey bird in the branches.

'Is it possible!' said the Lord-in-Waiting. 'I had never supposed it would look like that. How very plain it looks! It has certainly lost its colour from seeing so many grand folk here.'

'Little Nightingale,' called out the little kitchen-maid, 'our gracious Emperor wishes you to sing for him.'

'With the greatest pleasure,' said the Nightingale, and it sang, and it was a joy to hear it.

'It sounds like little glass bells,' said the Lord-in-Waiting; 'and just look at its little throat, how it moves! It is astonishing to think we have never heard it before! It will have a real *success* at Court.'

'Shall I sing for the Emperor again?' asked the Nightingale, who thought that the Emperor was there in person.

'Mine excellent little Nightingale,' said the Lord-in-Waiting, 'I have the great pleasure of bidding you to a Court-

Festival this night, when you will enchant His Imperial Majesty with your delightful warbling.'

'My voice sounds better among the green trees,' said the Nightingale. But it came willingly when it knew that the Emperor wished it.

There was a great deal of furbishing up at the palace. The walls and ceiling which were of porcelain, shone with the light of a thousand golden lamps. The most beautiful flowers of the tinkling kind were placed in the passages. There was a running to and fro and a great draught, but that is just what made the bells ring, and one could not hear oneself speak. In the middle of the great hall where the Emperor sat, a golden rod had been set up on which the Nightingale was to perch. The whole Court was present, and the little kitchen-maid was allowed to stand behind the door, for she had now the actual title of Court Kitchen-Maid. All were there in their smartest clothes, and they all looked toward the little grey bird to which the Emperor nodded.

And then the Nightingale sang, so gloriously that tears sprang into the Emperor's eyes and rolled down his cheeks, and the Nightingale sang even more sweetly. The song went straight to the heart, and the Emperor was so delighted that he declared that the Nightingale should have his golden slipper to hang round its neck. But the Nightingale declined. It had already had its reward.

'I have seen tears in the Emperor's eyes. That is my greatest reward. An Emperor's tears have a wonderful power. God knows I am sufficiently rewarded,' and again its sweet, glorious voice was heard.

'That is the most delightful coquetting I have ever known,' said the ladies sitting round, and they took water into their mouths, in order to gurgle when anyone spoke to them, and they really thought they were like the Nightingale. Even the footmen and the chambermaids sent word that they were satisfied, and that means a great deal, for they are always the most difficult people to please. Yes, indeed, there was no doubt as to the Nightingale's success. It was to stay at Court, and have its own cage, with liberty to go out twice in the day-time, and once at night. Twelve footmen went out with it, and each held a silk ribbon which was tied to the bird's leg, and which they held very tightly. There was not much pleasure in an outing of that sort. The whole town was talk-ing about the wonderful bird, and when two people met, one said: 'Nightin——' and the other said 'gale,' and they sighed and understood one another. Eleven cheesemongers' children were called after the bird, though none of them could sing a note.

One day a large parcel came for the Emperor. Outside was written the word: 'Nightingale.'

'Here we have a new book about our wonderful bird,' said the Emperor. But it was not a book; it was a little work of art which lay in a box—an artificial Nightingale, which looked exactly like the real one, but it was studded all over with diamonds, rubies and sapphires. As soon as you wound it up, it could sing one of the songs which the real bird sang, and its tail moved up and down and glittered with silver and gold. Round its neck was a ribbon on which was written: 'The Emperor of Japan's Nightingale is poor indeed, com-pared with the Emperor of China's.'

'That is delightful,' they all said, and on the messenger who had brought the artificial bird, they bestowed the title of 'Imperial Nightingale-Bringer-in-Chief.'

'Let them sing together, and *what* a duet that will be!'

And so they had to sing, but the thing would not work, because the real Nightingale could only sing in its own way, and the artificial Nightingale went by clockwork.

'That is not its fault,' said the band-master. 'Time is its strong point and it has quite my method.'

Then the artificial Nightingale had to sing alone. It had just as much success as the real bird, and it was so much handsomer to look at; it glittered like bracelets and breast-pins. It sang the same tune three and thirty times, and still it was not tired; the people would willingly listen to the whole performance over again from the start, but the Emperor suggested that the real Nightingale should sing for a while—where was it? Nobody had noticed it had flown out of the open window back to its green woods.

'But what is the meaning of all this?' said the Emperor. All the courtiers railed at the Nightingale and said it was a most ungrateful creature.

'We have the better of the two,' they said, and the artificial Nightingale had to sing again, and this was the thirty-fourth time they had heard the same tune. But they did not know it properly even then, because it was so difficult, and the band-master praised the wonderful bird in the highest terms and even asserted that it was superior to the real bird, not only as regarded the outside, with the many lovely diamonds, but the inside as well.

'You see, ladies and gentlemen, and above all your Imperial Majesty, that with the real Nightingale, you can never predict what may happen, but with the artificial bird, everything is settled beforehand; so it remains and it cannot be changed. One can account for it. One can rip it open, and show the human ingenuity, explaining how the cylinders lie, how they work, and how one thing is the result of another.'

'That is just what we think,' they all exclaimed, and the band-master received permission to exhibit the bird to the people on the following Sunday. The Emperor said they would hear it sing. They listened, and were as much delighted as if they had been drunk with tea, which is Chinese, you know, and they all said: 'Oh!' and stuck their forefingers in the air, and nodded their heads. But the poor fisherman who had heard the real Nightingale, said: 'It sounds quite well, and a little like it, but there is something wanting, I do not know what.'

The real Nightingale was banished from the Kingdom.

The artificial bird had its place on a silken cushion close to the Emperor's bed. All the presents it had received, the gold and precious stones, lay all round it, and it had been honoured with the title of High-Imperial-Bed-Room-Singer—in the first rank, on the left side, for even the Emperor considered that side the grander on which the heart is placed, and even an Emperor has his heart on the left side.

The band-master wrote twenty-five volumes about the wonderful artificial bird. The book was very learned and very long, filled with the most difficult words in the Chinese language, and everybody said they had read and understood it, for otherwise they would have been considered stupid, and would have been trampled upon.

And thus a whole year passed away. The Emperor, the Court, and all the Chinamen knew every little gurgle in the artificial bird's song, and just for this reason, they were all the better pleased with it. They could sing it themselves—which they did.

The boys in the street sang 'Zi-zi-zi', and 'cluck, cluck,' and even the Emperor sang it. Yes, it was certainly beautiful!

But one evening, while the bird was singing, and the Emperor lay in bed listening to it, there was a whirring sound inside the bird, and something whizzed; all the wheels ran round, and the music stopped.

The Emperor sprang out of bed and sent for the Court Physician, but what could he do? Then they sent for the watch-maker, and after much talk and examination, he patched the bird up, but he said it must be spared as much as possible, because the hammers were so worn out—and he could not put new ones in so that the music could be counted on. This was a great grief. The bird could only be allowed to sing once a year, and even that was risky, but on these occasions, the band-master would make a little speech, full of difficult words, saying the bird was just as good as ever—and that was true.

Five years passed away, and a great sorrow had come to the country. The people all really cared for their Emperor, and now he was ill and it was said he could not live. A new Emperor had been chosen, and the people stood about the streets, and questioned the Lord-in-Waiting about their Emperor's condition.

'P!' he said, and shook his head.

The Emperor lay pale and cold on his great, gorgeous bed; the whole Court believed that he was dead, and they all hastened to pay homage to the new Emperor. The footmen hurried off to discuss matters, and the chambermaids gave a great coffee-party. Cloth had been laid down in all the rooms and passages, so that not a footstep should be heard and it was all so very quiet. But the Emperor was not yet dead. He lay stiff and pale in the sumptuous bed, with its long velvet curtains and heavy gold tassels; high above was an open window, and the moon shone in upon the Emperor and the artificial bird. The poor Emperor could hardly breathe; he felt as if someone were sitting on his chest; he opened his eyes and saw that it was Death sitting on his chest, wearing his golden crown, holding in one hand his golden sword, and in the other his splendid banner. And from the folds of the velvet curtains strange faces peered forth; some terrible to look on, others mild and friendly—these were the Emperor's good and bad deeds, which gazed upon him now that Death sat upon his heart.

'Do you remember this?' whispered one after the other. 'Do you remember that?' They told him so much that the sweat poured down his face.

'I never knew that,' said the Emperor. 'Music! music! Beat the great Chinese drum!' he called out, 'so that I may not hear what they are saying!'

But they kept on, and Death nodded his head, like a China-man, at everything they said.

'Music, music,' cried the Emperor. 'You precious little golden bird! Sing to me, ah! sing to me! I have given you gold and costly treasures. I have hung my golden slipper about your neck. Sing to me. Sing to me!'

But the bird was silent; there was no one to wind him up, and therefore he could not sing. Death went on, staring at the Emperor with his great hollow eyes, and it was terribly still.

Then, suddenly, close to the window, came the sound of a lovely song. It was the little live Nightingale perched on a branch outside. It had heard of its Emperor's need, and had therefore flown hither to bring him comfort and hope, and as he sang, the faces became paler and the blood coursed more freely through the Emperor's veins. Even Death himself listened and said: 'Go on, little Nightingale. Go on.'

'Yes, if you will give me the splendid sword. Yes, if you will give me the Imperial banner! Yes, if you will give me the Emperor's crown!'

And Death gave back all these treasures for a song. And still the Nightingale sang on. He sang of the quiet church-yard, where the white roses grow, where the elder flowers bloom, and where the grass is kept moist by the tears of those left behind, and there came to Death such a longing to see his garden, that he floated out of the window, like a cold white mist.

'Thank you, thank you,' said the Emperor. 'You heavenly little bird, I know you well! I banished you from the land, and you have charmed away the evil spirits from my bed and you have driven Death from my heart. How shall I reward you?'

'You have rewarded me,' said the Nightingale. 'I brought tears to your eyes the first time I sang, and I shall never forget that. Those are the jewels which touched the heart of the singer; but sleep now, that you may wake fresh and strong.

I will sing to you.' Then it sang again, and the Emperor fell into a sweet sleep.

The sun shone in upon him through the window, when he woke the next morning feeling strong and well. None of his servants had come back, because they thought he was dead, but the Nightingale was still singing.

'You will always stay with me,' said the Emperor. 'You shall only sing when it pleases you, and I will break the arti-ficial Nightingale into a thousand pieces.'

'Do not do that,' said the Nightingale. 'It has done the best it could. Keep it with you. I cannot build my nest in a palace, but let me come just as I please. I will sit on the branch near the window, and sing to you that you may be both joy-ful and thoughtful. I will sing to you of the happy folk and of those that suffer; I will sing of the evil and of the good, which is being hidden from you. The little singing bird flies hither and thither, to the poor fisherman, to the peasant's hut, to many who live far from you and the Court. Your heart is dearer to me than your crown, and yet the crown has a breath of sanctity, too. I will come, I will sing to you! But one thing you must promise me!'

'All that you ask,' said the Emperor, and stood there in his imperial robes which he had put on himself, and held the heavy golden sword on his heart.

'I beg you, let no one know that you have a little bird who tells you everything. It will be far better so!'

Then the Nightingale flew away.

The servants came to look upon their dead Emperor. Yes, there they stood; and the Emperor said: 'Good morning!'

Hans Christian Andersen, freely translated from the Danish by Marie L. Shedlock, *The Art of the Storyteller* (Appleton-Century, N.Y.)

(See Note, page 222)

Where Love Is, God Is

In a certain town there lived a cobbler, Martin Avdéitch by
name. He had a tiny room in a basement, the one window of
which looked out onto the street. Through it one could only
see the feet of those who passed by, but Martin recognized
the people by their boots. He had lived long in the place and
had many acquaintances. There was hardly a pair of boots in
the neighbourhood that had not been once or twice through
his hands, so he often saw his own handiwork through the
window. Some he had re-soled, some patched, some stitched
up, and to some he had even put fresh uppers. He had plenty
to do, for he worked well, used good material, did not charge
too much, and could be relied on. If he could do a job by the day
required, he undertook it; if not, he told the truth and gave
no false promises; so he was well known and never short of
work.

Martin had always been a good man; but in his old age he
began to think more about his soul and to draw nearer to
God. While he still worked for a master, before he set up on
his own account, his wife had died, leaving him with a three-
year-old son. None of his elder children had lived, they had
all died in infancy. At first Martin thought of sending his
little son to his sister's in the country, but then he felt sorry
to part with the boy, thinking: 'It would be hard for my
little Kapitón to have to grow up in a strange family; I will
keep him with me.'

Martin left his master and went into lodgings with his
little son. But he had no luck with his children. No sooner
had the boy reached an age when he could help his father
and be a support as well as a joy to him, than he fell ill and,

after being laid up for a week with a burning fever, died. Martin buried his son, and gave way to despair so great and overwhelming that he murmured against God. In his sorrow he prayed again and again that he too might die, reproaching God for having taken the son he loved, his only son, while he, old as he was, remained alive. After that Martin left off going to church.

One day an old man from Martin's native village, who had been a pilgrim for the last eight years, called in on his way from Tróitsa Monastery. Martin opened his heart to him, and told him of his sorrow.

'I no longer even wish to live, holy man,' he said. 'All I ask of God is that I soon may die. I am now quite without hope in the world.'

The old man replied: 'You have no right to say such things, Martin. We cannot judge God's ways. Not our reasoning, but God's will, decides. If God willed that your son should die and you should live, it must be best so. As to your despair— that comes because you wish to live for your own happiness.'

'What else should one live for?' asked Martin.

'For God, Martin,' said the old man. 'He gives you life and you must live for Him. When you have learnt to live for Him, you will grieve no more, and all will seem easy to you.'

Martin was silent awhile, and then asked: 'But how is one to live for God?'

The old man answered: 'How one may live for God has been shown us by Christ. Can you read? Then buy the Gospels, and read them: there you will see how God would have you live. You have it all there.'

These words sank deep into Martin's heart, and that same day he went and bought himself a Testament in large print, and began to read.

At first he meant only to read on holidays, but having once begun he found it made his heart so light that he read every day. Sometimes he was so absorbed in his reading that the oil

in his lamp burnt out before he could tear himself away from
the book. He continued to read every night, and the more he
read the more clearly he understood what God required of
him, and how he might live for God. And his heart grew
lighter and lighter. Before, when he went to bed he used to
lie with a heavy heart, moaning as he thought of his little
Kapitón; but now he only repeated again and again: 'Glory
to Thee, glory to Thee, O Lord! Thy will be done!'

From that time Martin's whole life changed. Formerly, on
holidays he used to go and have tea at the public-house, and
did not even refuse a glass or two of vódka. Sometimes, after
having had a drop with a friend, he left the public-house not
drunk, but rather merry, and would say foolish things:
shout at a man, or abuse him. Now, all that sort of thing
passed away from him. His life became peaceful and joyful. He
sat down to his work in the morning, and when he had
finished his day's work he took the lamp down from the wall,
stood it on the table, fetched his book from the shelf, opened
it, and sat down to read. The more he read the better he
understood, and the clearer and happier he felt in his mind.

It happened once that Martin sat up late, absorbed in his
book. He was reading Luke's Gospel; and in the sixth
chapter he came upon the verses:

'To him that smiteth thee on the one cheek offer also the
other; and from him that taketh away thy cloke withhold
not thy coat also. Give to every man that asketh thee; and
of him that taketh away thy goods ask them not again. And
as ye would that men should do to you, do ye also to them
likewise.'

He also read the verses where our Lord says:

'And why call ye me, Lord, Lord, and do not the things
which I say? Whosoever cometh to me, and heareth my sayings, and doeth them, I will shew you to whom he is like:
He is like a man which built a house, and digged deep, and
laid the foundation on a rock : and when the flood arose, the

stream beat vehemently upon that house, and could not shake
it: for it was founded upon a rock. But he that heareth, and
doeth not, is like a man that without a foundation built an
house upon the earth, against which the stream did beat

vehemently, and immediately it fell; and the ruin of that
house was great.'

When Martin read these words his soul was glad within
him. He took off his spectacles and laid them on the book, and
leaning his elbows on the table pondered over what he had
read. He tried his own life by the standard of those words,
asking himself:

'Is my house built on the rock, or on sand? If it stands on
the rock, it is well. It seems easy enough while one sits here

alone, and one thinks one has done all that God commands;
but as soon as I cease to be on my guard, I sin again. Still I
will persevere. It brings such joy. Help me, O Lord!'

He thought all this, and was about to go to bed, but was
loth to leave his book. So he went on reading the seventh
chapter—about the centurion, the widow's son, and the answer to John's disciples—and he came to the part where a
rich Pharisee invited the Lord to his house; and he read how
the woman who was a sinner, anointed his feet and washed
them with her tears, and how he justified her. Coming to the
forty-fourth verse, he read:

'And turning to the woman, he said unto Simon, Seest thou
this woman? I entered into thine house, thou gavest me no
water for my feet: but she hath wetted my feet with her
tears, and wiped them with her hair. Thou gavest me no
kiss; but she, since the time I came in, hath not ceased to kiss
my feet. My head with oil thou didst not anoint: but she
hath anointed my feet with ointment.'

He read these verses and thought: 'He gave no water for
his feet, gave no kiss, his head with oil he did not anoint . . .'
And Martin took off his spectacles once more, laid them on
his book, and pondered.

'He must have been like me, that Pharisee. He too thought
only of himself—how to get a cup of tea, how to keep warm
and comfortable; never a thought of his guest. He took care
of himself, but for his guest he cared nothing at all. Yet who
was the guest? The Lord himself! If he came to me, should I
behave like that?'

Then Martin laid his head upon both his arms and, before
he was aware of it, he fell asleep.

'Martin!' he suddenly heard a voice, as if someone had
breathed the word above his ear.

He started from his sleep. 'Who's there?' he asked.

He turned round and looked at the door; no one was there.
He called again. Then he heard quite distinctly: 'Martin,

Martin! Look out into the street to-morrow, for I shall come.'

Martin roused himself, rose from his chair and rubbed his eyes, but did not know whether he had heard these words in a dream or awake. He put out the lamp and lay down to sleep.

Next morning he rose before daylight, and after saying his prayers he lit the fire and prepared his cabbage soup and buckwheat porridge. Then he lit the samovár, put on his apron, and sat down by the window to his work. As he sat working Martin thought over what had happened the night before. At times it seemed to him like a dream, and at times he thought that he had really heard the voice. 'Such things have happened before now,' thought he.

So he sat by the window, looking out into the street more than he worked, and whenever any one passed in unfamiliar boots he would stoop and look up, so as to see not the feet only but the face of the passer-by as well. A house-porter passed in new felt boots; then a water-carrier. Presently an old soldier of Nicholas' reign came near the window, spade in hand. Martin knew him by his boots, which were shabby old felt ones, goloshed with leather. The old man was called Stepánitch: a neighbouring tradesman kept him in his house for charity, and his duty was to help the house-porter. He began to clear away the snow before Martin's window. Martin glanced at him and then went on with his work.

'I must be growing crazy with age,' said Martin, laughing at his fancy. 'Stepánitch comes to clear away the snow, and I must needs imagine it's Christ coming to visit me. Old dotard that I am!'

Yet after he had made a dozen stitches he felt drawn to look out of the window again. He saw that Stepánitch had leaned his spade against the wall, and was either resting himself or trying to get warm. The man was old and broken down, and had evidently not enough strength even to clear away the snow.

'What if I called him in and gave him some tea?' thought Martin. 'The samovár is just on the boil.'

He stuck his awl in its place and rose; and putting the samovár on the table, made tea. Then he tapped the window with his fingers. Stepánitch turned and came to the window. Martin beckoned to him to come in, and went himself to open the door.

'Come in,' he said, 'and warm yourself a bit. I'm sure you must be cold.'

'May God bless you!' Stepánitch answered. 'My bones do ache to be sure.' He came in, first shaking off the snow, and lest he should leave marks on the floor he began wiping his feet; but as he did so he tottered and nearly fell.

'Don't trouble to wipe your feet,' said Martin; 'I'll wipe up the floor—it's all in the day's work. Come, friend, sit down and have some tea.'

Filling two tumblers, he passed one to his visitor, and pouring his own out into the saucer, began to blow on it.

Stepánitch emptied his glass, and, turning it upside down, put the remains of his piece of sugar on the top. He began to express his thanks, but it was plain that he would be glad of some more.

'Have another glass,' said Martin, refilling the visitor's tumbler and his own. But while he drank his tea Martin kept looking out into the street.

'Are you expecting any one?' asked the visitor.

'Am I expecting any one? Well, now, I'm ashamed to tell you. It isn't that I really expect any one; but I heard something last night which I can't get out of my mind. Whether it was a vision, or only a fancy, I can't tell. You see, friend, last night I was reading the Gospel, about Christ the Lord, how he suffered, and how he walked on earth. You have heard tell of it, I dare say.'

'I have heard tell of it,' answered Stepánitch; 'but I'm an ignorant man and not able to read.'

'Well, you see, I was reading of how he walked on earth. I came to that part, you know, where he went to a Pharisee who did not receive him well. Well, friend, as I read about it, I thought how that man did not receive Christ the Lord with proper honour. Suppose such a thing could happen to such a man as myself, I thought, what would I not do to receive him! But that man gave him no reception at all. Well, friend, as I was thinking of this, I began to doze, and as I dozed I heard some one call me by name. I got up and thought I heard some one whispering, "Expect me; I will come to-morrow." This happened twice over. And to tell you the truth, it sank so into my mind that, though I am ashamed of it myself, I keep on expecting him, the dear Lord!'

Stepánitch shook his head in silence, finished his tumbler and laid it on its side; but Martin stood it up again and re-filled it for him.

'Here, drink another glass, bless you! And I was thinking, too, how he walked on earth and despised no one, but went mostly among common folk. He went with plain people, and chose his disciples from among the likes of us, from workmen like us, sinners that we are. "He who raises himself," he said, "shall be humbled; and he who humbles himself shall be raised." " You call me Lord," he said, "and I will wash your feet." "He who would be first," he said, "let him be the servant of all; because," he said, "blessed are the poor, the humble, the meek, and the merciful."'

Stepánitch forgot his tea. He was an old man, easily moved to tears, and as he sat and listened the tears ran down his cheeks.

'Come, drink some more,' said Martin. But Stepánitch crossed himself, thanked him, moved away his tumbler, and rose.

'Thank you, Martin Avdéitch,' he said, 'you have given me food and comfort both for soul and body.'

'You're very welcome. Come again another time. I am glad to have a guest,' said Martin.

Stepánitch went away; and Martin poured out the last of the tea and drank it up. Then he put away the tea things and sat down to his work, stitching the back seam of a boot. And as he stitched he kept looking out of the window, waiting for Christ, and thinking about him and his doings. And his head was full of Christ's sayings.

Two soldiers went by: one in Government boots, the other in boots of his own; then the master of a neighbouring house, in shining goloshes; then a baker carrying a basket. All these passed on. Then a woman came up in worsted stockings and peasant-made shoes. She passed the window, but stopped by the wall. Martin glanced up at her through the window, and saw that she was a stranger, poorly dressed, and with a baby in her arms. She stopped by the wall with her back to the wind, trying to wrap the baby up though she had hardly anything to wrap it in. The woman had only summer clothes on, and even they were shabby and worn. Through the window Martin heard the baby crying, and the woman trying to soothe it, but unable to do so. Martin rose, and going out of the door and up the steps he called to her.

'My dear, I say, my dear!'

The woman heard, and turned round.

'Why do you stand out there with the baby in the cold? Come inside. You can wrap him up better in a warm place. Come this way!'

The woman was surprised to see an old man in an apron, with spectacles on his nose, calling to her, but she followed him in.

They went down the steps, entered the little room, and the old man led her to the bed.

'There, sit down, my dear, near the stove. Warm yourself, and feed the baby.'

'Haven't any milk. I have eaten nothing myself since early

morning,' said the woman, but still she took the baby to her breast.

Martin shook his head. He brought out a basin and some bread. Then he opened the oven door and poured some cabbage soup into the basin. He took out the porridge pot also, but the porridge was not yet ready, so he spread a cloth on the table and served only the soup and bread.

'Sit down and eat, my dear, and I'll mind the baby. Why, bless me, I've had children of my own; I know how to manage them.'

The woman crossed herself, and sitting down at the table began to eat, while Martin put the baby on the bed and sat down by it. He chucked and chucked, but having no teeth he could not do it well and the baby continued to cry. Then Martin tried poking at him with his finger; he drove his finger straight at the baby's mouth and then quickly drew it back, and did this again and again. He did not let the baby take his finger to its mouth, because it was all black with cobbler's wax. But the baby first grew quiet watching the finger, and then began to laugh. And Martin felt quite pleased.

The woman sat eating and talking, and told him who she was, and where she had been.

'I'm a soldier's wife,' said she. 'They sent my husband somewhere, far away, eight months ago, and I have heard nothing of him since. I had a place as cook till my baby was born, but then they would not keep me with a child. For three months now I have been struggling, unable to find a place, and I've had to sell all I had for food. I tried to go as a wet-nurse, but no one would have me; they said I was too starved-looking and thin. Now I have just been to see a tradesman's wife (a woman from our village is in service with her) and she has promised to take me. I thought it was all settled at last, but she tells me not to come till next week. It is far to her place, and I am fagged out, and baby is quite starved, poor mite. Fortunately our landlady has pity on us, and lets us lodge free, else I don't know what we should do.'

Martin sighed. 'Haven't you any warmer clothing?' he asked.

'How could I get warm clothing?' said she. 'Why, I pawned my last shawl for sixpence yesterday.'

Then the woman came and took the child, and Martin got up. He went and looked among some things that were hang-ing on the wall, and brought back an old cloak.

'Here,' he said, 'though it's a worn-out old thing, it will do to wrap him up in.'

The woman looked at the cloak, then at the old man, and taking it, burst into tears. Martin turned away, and groping under the bed brought out a small trunk. He fumbled about in it, and again sat down opposite the woman. And the woman said:

'The Lord bless you, friend. Surely Christ must have sent me to your window, else the child would have frozen. It was mild when I started, but now see how cold it has turned. Surely it must have been Christ who made you look out of your window and take pity on me, poor wretch!'

Martin smiled and said, 'It is quite true; it was he made me do it. It was no mere chance made me look out.'

And he told the woman his dream, and how he had heard the Lord's voice promising to visit him that day.

'Who knows? All things are possible,' said the woman. And she got up and threw the cloak over her shoulders, wrapping it round herself and round the baby. Then she bowed, and thanked Martin once more.

'Take this for Christ's sake,' said Martin, and gave her sixpence to get her shawl out of pawn. The woman crossed herself, and Martin did the same, and then he saw her out.

After the woman had gone, Martin ate some cabbage soup, cleared the things away, and sat down to work again. He sat and worked, but did not forget the window, and every time a shadow fell on it he looked up at once to see who was passing. People he knew and strangers passed by, but no one remarkable.

After a while Martin saw an apple-woman stop just in front of his window. She had a large basket, but there did not seem to be many apples left in it; she had evidently sold most of her stock. On her back she had a sack full of chips, which she was taking home. No doubt she had gathered them at some place where building was going on. The sack evidently hurt her, and she wanted to shift it from one shoulder to the other, so she put it down on the footpath and, placing her basket on a post, began to shake down the chips in the sack. While she was doing this a boy in a tattered cap ran up, snatched an apple out of the basket, and tried to slip away; but the old woman noticed it, and turning, caught the boy by his sleeve. He began to struggle, trying to free himself, but the old woman held on with both hands, knocked his cap off his head, and seized hold of his hair. The boy screamed and the old woman scolded. Martin dropped his awl, not waiting to stick it in its place, and rushed out of the door. Stumbling up the steps, and dropping his spectacles in his hurry, he ran out into the street. The old woman was pulling the boy's hair and scolding him, and threatening to take him to the police. The lad was struggling and protesting, saying, 'I did not take it. What are you beating me for? Let me go!'

Martin separated them. He took the boy by the hand and said, 'Let him go, Granny. Forgive him for Christ's sake.'

'I'll pay him out, so that he won't forget it for a year! I'll take the rascal to the police!'

Martin began entreating the old woman.

'Let him go, Granny. He won't do it again. Let him go for Christ's sake!'

The old woman let go, and the boy wished to run away, but Martin stopped him.

'Ask the Granny's forgiveness!' said he. 'And don't do it another time. I saw you take the apple.'

The boy began to cry and to beg pardon.

'That's right. And now here's an apple for you,' and Martin took an apple from the basket and gave it to the boy, saying, 'I will pay you, Granny.'

'You will spoil them that way, the young rascals,' said the old woman. 'He ought to be whipped so that he should re-member it for a week.'

'Oh, Granny, Granny,' said Martin, 'that's our way—but it's not God's way. If he should be whipped for stealing an apple, what should be done to us for our sins?'

The old woman was silent.

And Martin told her the parable of the lord who forgave his servant a large debt, and how the servant went out and seized his debtor by the throat. The old woman listened to it all, and the boy, too, stood by and listened.

'God bids us forgive,' said Martin, 'or else we shall not be forgiven. Forgive every one; and a thoughtless youngster most of all.'

The old woman wagged her head and sighed.

'It's true enough,' said she, 'but they are getting terribly spoilt.'

'Then we old ones must show them better ways,' Martin replied.

'That's just what I say,' said the old woman. 'I have had seven of them myself, and only one daughter is left.' And the old woman began to tell how and where she was living with her daughter, and how many grandchildren she had. 'There now,' she said, 'I have but little strength left, yet I work hard for the sake of my grandchildren; and nice children they are, too. No one comes out to meet me but the children. Little Annie, now, won't leave me for any one. "It's grand-mother, dear grandmother, darling grandmother."' And the old woman completely softened at the thought.

'Of course, it was only his childishness, God help him,' said she, referring to the boy.

As the old woman was about to hoist her sack on her back, the lad sprang forward to her, saying, 'Let me carry it for you, Granny. I'm going that way.'

The old woman nodded her head, and put the sack on the boy's back, and they went down the street together, the old woman quite forgetting to ask Martin to pay for the apple. Martin stood and watched them as they went along talking to each other.

When they were out of sight Martin went back to the house. Having found his spectacles unbroken on the steps, he picked up his awl and sat down again to work. He worked a little, but could soon not see to pass the bristle through the holes in the leather; and presently he noticed the lamp-lighter passing on his way to light the street lamps.

'Seems it's time to light up,' thought he. So he trimmed his lamp, hung it up, and sat down again to work. He finished off one boot and, turning it about, examined it. It was all right. Then he gathered his tools together, swept up the cuttings, put away the bristles and the thread and the awls, and, taking down the lamp, placed it on the table. Then he took the Gospels from the shelf. He meant to open them at the place he had marked the day before with a bit of morocco, but the book opened at another place. As Martin opened it, his yesterday's dream came back to his mind, and no sooner had he thought of it than he seemed to hear footsteps, as though some one were moving behind him. Martin turned round, and it seemed to him as if people were standing in the dark corner, but he could not make out who they were. And a voice whispered in his ear: 'Martin, Martin, don't you know me?'

'Who is it?' muttered Martin.

'It is I,' said the voice. And out of the dark corner stepped

Stepánitch, who smiled and vanishing like a cloud was seen no more.

'It is I,' said the voice again. And out of the darkness stepped the woman with the baby in her arms, and the woman smiled and the baby laughed, and they too vanished.

'It is I,' said the voice once more. And the old woman and the boy with the apple stepped out and both smiled, and then they too vanished.

And Martin's soul grew glad. He crossed himself, put on his spectacles, and began reading the Gospel just where it had opened; and at the top of the page he read:

'I was an hungred, and ye gave me meat: I was thirsty, and ye gave me drink: I was a stranger, and ye took me in.'

And at the bottom of the page he read:

'Inasmuch as ye did it unto one of these my brethren, even these least, ye did it unto me' (Matt. *xxv*).

And Martin understood that his dream had come true; and that the Saviour had really come to him that day, and he had welcomed him.

From *Twenty-Three Tales by Tolstoy* translated by Aylmer Maude (Oxford University Press, London)

(See Note, page 223)

For the Storyteller

For the Storyteller

Storytelling is an art but one that, given the desire to succeed, may be acquired through practice and experience. Each one of us is a potential storyteller for we can all relate our own experiences with enthusiasm, conviction and a wealth of detail. This is because we are interested in what happens to ourselves, we have *seen* it happen and we want to tell others about it. Here are the essentials for successful storytelling, identification with what we tell, a clear picture of events and a desire to share the story with others.

Even in these days of the making and reading of many books, the story that is told by word of mouth holds its own. The spoken word is the memorable word and the voice and personality of the storyteller add richness to the story and lift it from the printed page into life.

All the stories in this book have given pleasure not only to countless listeners but also to me, for the first principle of choosing a story to tell is that it should appeal strongly to the storyteller. If it does not, he will tell it without conviction and the audience may well receive it with indifference. Every storyteller has to recognise that there are some stories that will never be his, although someone else may tell them with enthusiasm and success.

Whether stories should be learnt by heart, word for word, or told in one's own words, is a question I am often asked. This depends on both the storyteller and the story. It is easier for some people to learn a story by heart than to put it into their own words, others find it hampering to be confined to the actual words of the book. But the story itself must also be taken into consideration. There are some stories that have been told so perfectly by masters of their craft that there is no other way in which to tell them. So no one would use any but Rumer Godden's words for *The Mousewife* or Rudyard Kipling's for *Just So Stories* and the stories of Hans Andersen, provided a good translation is used, should be told as they are written. Traditional folk and fairy tales are in the perfect form for telling for they have been handed down orally from generation to generation.

When the time comes to choose a story, it is important to remember that not every story we read and like is suitable for telling, for what appeals to the eye and the mind may not appeal equally to the ear and the imagination. For effective telling the story must be direct and rich in action. Stories that are obviously unsuitable for telling as they stand should not be chosen by the inexperienced storyteller, but left until experience has given skill in adaptation.

Choose for your first stories to tell, therefore, those which are simple and dramatic and written in a suitable form for telling, as for example, *Lazy Tok* and *The Magic Tea-Kettle* in this book. There is a wealth of material in folk tale collections like those of Joseph Jacobs—*Mr Vinegar, Tom Tit Tot*—or *Salt* and *Baba Yaga* in Arthur Ransome's *Old Peter's Russian Tales*. Wanda Gag's versions of Grimm's stories are just right for telling, as are also Andersen's simpler tales *The Tinder-Box* or *The Swineherd*. Once successful tellings have given confidence, the storyteller can experiment with different types of stories to find those that suit him best. For some it may be 'hero stories' such as Beowulf, King Arthur or Roland; for others fantasy by modern authors or realistic adventure as in *Jim Davis*, Masefield's smuggling story for boys. The scope for choice of stories is very wide and storytellers will find it useful to note down possible stories to tell as they come across them in their reading.

It is important that a storyteller should know a few stories really well as soon as possible. Librarians, teachers and others

who tell stories are often asked for one at a moment's notice.
If they can tell a story that is suitable for a mixed audience of
adults and children, so much the better. Wanda Gag's *Gone
is Gone*, Andersen's *The Nightingale* and even a simple story
like Rose Fyleman's *Magic Umbrella*, are suitable for this
purpose.

When the storyteller has had some experience, he will
find that there are some stories he would like to tell that
need adaptation in some way. The audience must be able to
follow the story easily, for there can be no turning back to
re-read as in a book. Descriptive passages have to be shortened,
unnecessary complications of the plot deleted, some passages
rephrased. Some of Barbara Leonie Picard's stories, for instance, which are good material for the storyteller, need this
kind of treatment.

The way in which a story begins is of the utmost import-
ance if it is to capture the child's interest and curiosity from
the first moment. An old folk tale starts, 'A poor boy once
hired himself out to a farmer for one marrow-fat pea a year',
and at once the child is intrigued. Children are amused by
the opening of *The Jolly Little Tailor*, for they cannot
imagine what could happen to such a very thin man. But
the first sentence in Andersen's *The Nightingale* appears
silly to children—of course the Emperor of China is a Chinaman!

Endings are equally important, for on these depends the
impression left on the child's mind when the story is done.
He should be left with a relaxed feeling of satisfaction for now
the hero and the heroine are happy, the battles are over, the
quest has been successful and right has triumphed. How
deeply pleasing to know that Elsie Piddock, to whom skipping means so much, will skip for ever in her sleep! Sometimes the feeling of finality can be achieved by the intonation
of the voice only, at other times the last paragraph may have
to be completely rephrased. Beware of the anti-climax when

the interest of the story is really over. Whatever else is left
to the inspiration of the moment, the first and last sentences
of a story must be always memorised.

There can be no hard or fast rule for *learning* a story. For
some memorising is no problem, for others it will be necessary
to evolve some individual method of absorbing a story. What
is *essential* is that the preparation is so thorough that when
faced by an audience, there can be no uncertainty or fumbling
for words.

A suggestion from long experience may be of help for the
storyteller who finds it difficult to master a story. First read
the story several times, carefully and with concentration.
Then jot down an outline from memory, noting the stages in
the development of the plot and the part the characters play.
Read the story again to discover the places where it has not
been clearly remembered. The secret of memorising a story,
as Ruth Sawyer has said in her *The Way of a Storyteller*,
and as all experienced storytellers know, is to *see* it as a series
of pictures. The background, the people, the events must all
be visualised before we can make others see them, too. In
the same way, if we are really inside the story and can feel its
mood, this will come over to those who listen. *Live* with the
story until it has been completely absorbed.

Now repeat the story *aloud*. Only in this way can we
realise the tricks our memory can play us. A good vocabulary
and an easy flow of words will help at this stage, but it is
surprising how these improve with practice and growing
confidence. The words we choose are as important as colours
to a painter, for they are the means by which we interpret
and give life to stories we love.

When the day comes on which the story is to be told to an
audience, there should be no nervousness as long as it has been
well chosen and prepared. We have something we want to
share, the children wait expectantly, prepared to enjoy the
story we have found for them. Remember to show them the

book from which it comes, for a well told story often sends the child back to read more.

Tell the story in a natural and relaxed way, for story-telling is not a dramatic performance. There is a place for gesture and change of voice to indicate character, but only if these can be introduced spontaneously and naturally. The storyteller has only his voice, his personality, his faith in the story he has to tell. It is for the hearer to imagine the scene, to set the stage, to visualise the characters through the story-teller's interpretation.

Give any necessary explanations before the story begins, remembering that the child's imagination and the context often supply the answer. So, in the tale of *Lazy Tok*, there is no need to describe a Nipah tree or a Booloodoopy (if one could). These are foreign sounding words which give atmo-sphere and it matters not at all what they really mean.

Make full use of the 'dramatic pause' before important events or at a climax. Children have quick minds and often guess what is going to happen, but a pause prolongs the sus-pense and gives the audience time to enjoy the pleasures of anticipation. Pace, too, is important, for timing is as vital in a story as in a play and can set the mood and strengthen the impact of what is happening. In 'Elsie Piddock', the words sometimes skip to the rhythm of the turning rope, but the Mousewife walks 'slowly and quietly' home to bed, for she has seen the stars.

The voice is our instrument and it should be pleasant to hear and flexible in expressing shades of feeling or character. To be inaudible is unforgiveable and renders all our prepara-tion useless. A few lessons on how to manage the voice with-out strain are invaluable. Technique can enable us to be heard anywhere, correct diction will ensure that we can be under-stood by anyone.

The stories in this book are a very individual choice. I have chosen them from the hundreds I have told because I have found that in them my own enjoyment of their fantasy and fun adds to the pleasure of the audience. This kind of story has become part of me, particularly the first story in the book, my favourite. Probably no other storyteller would make the same anthology.

But, whatever the story, if it is well chosen and carefully prepared it will give pleasure. As we tell it with warmth and enjoyment, we shall have our reward in the spontaneous response of the audience, whether it be laughter or emotion. 'In stories lies man's wisdom and knowledge and sense of beauty and wonder.'

EILEEN COLWELL

NOTES FOR THE STORYTELLER

Elsie Piddock Skips in her Sleep

Telling time: 25–30 minutes.
Audience: Children of all ages, particularly girls. Adults enjoy the story, too.
Occasion: A story for the 'skipping season' (Spring).
For the experienced storyteller.

This story is a delightful combination of reality and that 'extension of reality' that is fantasy. The tale of little Elsie Piddock who could skip 'as never so', is one that appeals to children and adults alike. From the first to the last moment, there is a feeling of enchantment.

The skipping rhyme must, of course, be repeated to the rhythm of an invisible skipping rope.

The story is a little long for telling and although one is reluctant to lose a word, it is possible to omit the description of Elsie's skipping feats during the year that she is learning to skip as the fairies skip. The struggle between the wicked Lord and the villagers can be summarised, as long as it remains clear that a factory is to be built on Mount Caburn, which means that the children—and the fairies—will have nowhere to skip at the new moon.

The Skipping Match is the culmination of all that goes before and must not be curtailed by a word. When the tiny, bent figure of Elsie Piddock steps out to skip and we see that she has the *fairy* rope in her hand, the listening children lean forward eagerly for they know something magical must happen. 'And do but see, she's skipping in her sleep!' cries Ellen Maltman, and it is this that gives the end of the story its dreamlike quality. The turning of the rope which we know must go on for ever and ever, becomes almost hypnotic, so that insensibly the storyteller speaks as though in a dream and the children *see* the tiny figure skipping . . . skipping . . . skipping . . . in its sleep.

A story full of the gaiety and verve of the author and a joy to tell.

The Swallow and the Mole

Telling time: 10 minutes.
Audience: Children of 8 upwards.
Easy to tell.

Storytelling still plays a very important part in the life of African villages. The stories in the book from which this tale comes, were told to the author by an old African and had been handed down in his tribe for generations. Geraldine Elliot in her turn has clothed the stories in her own words so that children of far off countries may enjoy them.

Characterisation is important in this story—the gentle, kindly and humble Mole, the bullying Elephant, the clever and grateful Swallow. Postpone the description of the *kind* of competition that is to be held until the animals have reached the meeting place, as this adds interest to the actual contest.

The end of the story could be improved for children. Surely the proud and happy Mole would have burst out with the news to his friend, rather than allow it to be told by Kamba. Swallow, too, would respond warmly to the friend to whom he owed so much. To give a feeling of warmth and to round off the story, try the following sentences :—

(Mole says) ' "*I* caught the ball three times—I don't know how I did it! I wish you had been there to see, Swallow."

Swallow smiled. "It must have been very exciting!" he said. "Fancy you being King, Mole! I *am* glad. You'll make a very good King."

And Mole and his friends went off happily together.'

Note that the name Mfuko is pronounced M'*foo*-koh and Namazeze, Nah-mah-*zeh*-zeh.

A Chinese Fairy Tale

Telling time: Between 20 and 25 minutes.
Audience: Children of 7–10 upwards and adults.
A difficult story to tell but an effective one for the experienced story-teller.

This is one of Laurence Housman's most effective and beautiful fantasies from *Moonshine and Clover*, written in 1923 and now out of print. It has imaginative power and an enchantment of atmosphere that never fails to move an audience.

Housman was trained as an artist and illustrated books before he wrote one himself. Hence his use of such artist's terms as 'linen-stretchers', 'mahl-stick'. The 'lakes and the cobalts' are, of course, the reds and the blues. Screwed up pellets of bread were used as erasers.

Some cuts are advisable. Omit the second sentence at the very beginning of the story—the reason will be obvious. Omit also the paragraph beginning, 'All that day they kept scratching their left ears . . .'

After we know that Wio-Wani has a brick in his hand, it is obvious what he will do with it, so omit from 'Down the garden path came Wio-Wani' to 'became his own tombstone', and say simply 'Wio-Wani threw the brick—and Tiki-Pu's master spoke no more.' This is enough, especially for children. Justice has been done.

As Tiki-Pu at the end of the story calls for the last time: 'O Wio-Wani, dear master, are you there?' there must be a pause as we *all* listen, followed by five words only, spoken without haste, 'But no voice answered him.' If the storyteller knows how to tell stories, there will be silence until the spell is broken at his own volition.

The Young Man with Music in his Fingers

Telling time: 25 minutes.
Audience: Children of 8–10 upwards.
For the experienced storyteller.

This is perhaps one of the best of Diana Ross's modern fairy stories. Although it seems to have a conventional and traditional fairy tale pattern, the author has transformed it into an original and absorbing story. The gifts the young man receives are so unusual that the listener is intrigued to know how they can possibly help him in his quest. The situations and characters are strongly dramatic and the ending satisfying, for the hero uses his gifts to make all the music for his own wedding.

The story will be too long for many occasions. It would be possible to summarise one of the quests, preferably that of the Ancient Maiden of the Sea as the least dramatic. Simply say that the young man with his second gift, twanging upon his fingers to make the sweet music of harps playing, charmed the Ancient Maiden of the Sea from her palace ten thousand fathoms under the sea so that she gave him the seven emeralds from her hair. Omit the Wise Woman's description of the perils he will meet on each quest—these will be evident when he meets them.

Once the youth has the wonderful crown, the end should come quickly. Omit the details of the ninety-nine suitors for the prize and allow the young man to march straight from the gate to the maiden so that he can give her the crown. The order of the last three paragraphs is wrong for dramatic effect. After 'So then they were married' omit all that goes before the final paragraph and end with that, for it is the culmination of the story.

Note the repetitive phrases and the flowing prose that is almost poetry at times. Here are the virtues one would wish to find in the hero of a children's story—kindness, courage and humility.

The Jolly Tailor who Became King

Telling time: 12 minutes.
Audience: Children of 7–9 upwards and adults.
A funny story that is easy to tell.

This amusing story from Poland comes from a collection that is not available in England. It was told in Polish and English to children in the New York libraries before it was written down in the nineteen-twenties. Its simple style, so fast moving and direct, is exactly right for the storyteller because of its folktale pattern.

Omit the strange piece of folklore about Mr Nitechka's visit to the devils' home. The story is complete without it. After 'He tied it again to his body' link the story with this sentence: 'After seven days of adventure, Nitechka and Count Scarecrow reached Patsanoff, a beautiful old town where the King had died. They were greatly astonished to see that all around the town it was sunshiny and pleasant, but over Patsanoff the rain poured from the sky as from a bucket . . .'

It is effective to insert a short paragraph to describe what happens while Mr Nitechka is darning the sky. As he mends the hole, the rain slackens and when he puts in the last stitch and presses the seam, the rain ceases altogether, the dogs run madly across the wet grass, smoke rises from the chimneys once more and the children

dance for joy in the sunshine. So, when the little tailor comes down
the ladder to become King, the scene is set for his triumph.

It is the personality of the jolly little tailor contrasted with that
of the self-important Count Scarecrow, that makes the story so
appealing. The elegant manners of the friends are not lost upon the
children who listen.

A story that is fun to tell.

The Selfish Giant

Telling time: 10 minutes.
Audience: Children of 7–10 upwards and adults.
Occasion: Easter or at any time when a story with a religious theme
is suitable.
Not difficult to tell.

Written in 1888, *The Selfish Giant* and *The Happy Prince* are the
best known of this sophisticated writer's stories and the most suitable
for children. For adults *The Selfish Giant* is an allegory, for children
a story only. It is full of pictures which the storyteller must see in his
imagination so that he can describe them to his audience. The
characters should be clearly imagined too—the gruff, clumsy Giant,
the laughing children, the radiant Child.

There is no need to shorten the story for telling for it is not long
and it can be easily memorised because of its flowing, musical style.
It should move happily and peacefully until the tempestuous return
of the Giant shatters the children's joy. Changes in voice and pace are
necessary as Winter and then Spring come to the garden and the Giant
sees and loves the Child. The last sentence of the story is not a gloomy
obituary notice, but a sign that at last the Giant has found his heart's
desire.

Suppose You Met a Witch

Telling time: 8 minutes.
Audience: Children of 7–9 upwards.
Occasion: Hallowe'en or when telling stories in the firelight.
Needs practice and a good reader.

Ian Serraillier is an outstanding poet of today for young people. His poems are written with reading aloud in mind. His approach to poetry is essentially modern and he uses unconventional forms of verse and contemporary idiom. His two long poems, *Everest is Climbed* and *The Ballad of Kon-tiki*, read aloud well.

Ian Serraillier often chooses a fairy tale theme for his narrative poems. *Suppose You Met a Witch* is based on one of Grimm's stories. Its use of alliteration and frequent change of rhythm and length of line, make it exciting for both the ear and the imagination. The form of the poem determines the pace and the way in which it should be spoken or read to be effective.

The Monster Who Grew Small

Telling time: 15 minutes.
Audience: Children of 7–9 upwards, especially boys.
Occasion: For use with groups of boys, for instance Wolf Cubs.
Not difficult to learn or tell.

This story comes from a collection, *The Scarlet Fish*, written by Joan Grant, author of several novels about ancient Egypt. It is not necessarily an authentic legend, but it might well have been enjoyed by children in the Egypt of long ago.

Take care not to give the boy his name Miobi, the Frightened One, until he does so himself, for the author has introduced it at exactly the right time for dramatic effect. A small point—children like to hear the serpents Miobi meets hiss realistically, an effect that can easily be achieved by a suitable choice of victims for them to name to each other, for example, 'S-s-sailor', 'Was-s-sherwoman', 'S-s-servant'.

The real climax of the story comes when Miobi finds that the Monster has grown small enough for him to take in his hand. The story should end as quickly as possible after this for all else is anti-climax. After the phrase 'the simmer of a cooking pot', therefore, continue thus:—

'Poor little Monster!' said Miobi. 'You must feel lonely in this big cave. What is your name?'

'Most people call me "What-Might-Happen",' said the Monster.

'You shall be my pet and I shall take you home with me,' said Miobi. 'Your fiery breath can light my cooking-fire.'

So Miobi took the Monster home. Never again did men call the boy Miobi, the Frightened One; they gave him a new name, The Slayer of Monsters.

This story with its lesson that courage cannot be given but must be won by facing up to difficulties, is one that is suitable for children anywhere and which will have the full approval of adults.

The Children of Lir

Telling time: 10 minutes.
Audience: Children of 9–11.
A straightforward story that is not difficult to tell.

It is said that as late as 1953 there were more good storytellers of traditional tales to be found in Galway than in the whole of Europe. Every village in Ireland used to have its *Shanachie* and some of these men and women could tell as many as 340 stories, some of great length. Old stories such as *The Children of Lir* would not have survived had it not been for the storytellers who passed them on for hundreds of years.

There were three 'Sorrows of Storytelling', great tragic tales, known to the Shanachie. *The Children of Lir* was the second and the others were *The Children of Turenn* and *The Children of Usnach*. Of the three this is the most moving and gentle and it should be told simply and quietly. In it we see an example of a pagan legend touched by the influence of Christianity. By the end of the story, the ancient gods of Ireland have shrunk to the stature of 'Sidhe', that is, 'The Fairy people who live in a mound', and Christianity has come to Ireland.

The relation between storyteller and audience was an intimate one and each person would feel that the story was being told to him personally. This is why I have suggested that someone is telling the story directly to an audience.

The Magic Tea-Kettle

Telling time: 12 minutes.
Audience: Children of any age.
An amusing and easy tale to tell.

A Japanese story retold by Rhoda Power so gaily that children enjoy it immensely. It is full of action and words that sound amusing. To children the 'Wiggle-waggle, bubble-bubble' theme is enormously funny.

The story should be told at a good pace, particularly when the badger-kettle begins to boil and rush round the room. Pause significantly before the tail and nose appear out of the kettle.

The author has written the story for telling to children, so its approach is direct and there is no need to omit anything. It may be, however, that the storyteller does not feel at ease with such phrases as, 'Please don't laugh . . . I'm not joking . . . I hardly like to tell you.' These need to be spontaneous and are perhaps better left to the inspiration of the moment.

An easy tale to tell and always a successful one.

The Midnight Folk

Telling time: 25 minutes.
Audience: Boys and girls of 8–12.
Occasion: To introduce Masefield's books to children.

John Masefield, a great storyteller, has said that his life work has been 'the finding, the framing and telling of stories'. He has written two fantasies for children, *The Midnight Folk* and *The Box of Delights*. In this extract from the first of these two books, we see many memories of his childhood. It is a dream story but there is nothing whimsy or insubstantial about it. It is the book not only of a storyteller but of a poet as we see from the imaginative descriptions of the underwater world.

Kay Harker, the boy in the story, is looking for the treasure lost by his great-grandfather Captain Harker. The legend is that Captain Harker was entrusted with the treasure of the churches of Santa Barbara at a time of revolution. But his crew mutinied, marooned their Captain and sailed away with the treasure. By the time Captain Harker was rescued and got back to England, all trace of the crew and the treasure had been lost. In the story each chapter reveals a little more of what happened to the treasure, until in the last chapter it is found and restored to its rightful owners.

The ship called the *Plunderer* was Captain Harker's ship. Abner Brown is the arch-villain of the story. He too is looking for the treasure, but for his own ends.

John Masefield's lively personality and sense of fun, his love of a story, his passion for the sea, his poet's eye for beauty, are all here in the story he is creating for his own pleasure and for his children. The details are those which children love, the adventures are a child's wish fulfilment, the imaginative use of words an enrichment and stimulation for the imagination of all children.

A Meal with a Magician

Telling time: 20 minutes.
Audience: Children of 8–10 upwards, particularly boys.
For an experienced storyteller.

Surely one of the essential qualities for a scientist is imagination, so it is no surprise to find a learned professor writing an amusing fantasy that sends children into fits of laughter by its understatement and puckish humour. The beginning is so ordinary and circumstantial that the absurdities that follow are all the more effective. The fish course is caught from the air by an octopus and grilled on the fiery paws of a little dragon wearing asbestos boots, and all that Mr Leakey says is, 'I don't know if you've noticed anything queer about this dinner . . .' This matter-of-fact attitude towards magic should be maintained by the storyteller.

Relate the story as a personal experience and tell it with a straight face—if possible. No detail of the food eaten should be omitted, for children love to hear about things to eat! Their appetite for the sound of long words is also considerable, so that the formal and flowery conversation between Mr Leakey and the Jinn is enjoyed and the final phrase, 'The like unto thee, with brazen knobs thereon,' often calls forth a snort of laughter.

The explanation of the origin of the starched shirt front can be omitted for children, as also the whole incident of Leopold the beetle. Omit also the first paragraph in the story and begin at 'When I first met Mr Leakey . . .'

This story comes from *My Friend Mr Leakey* by J. B. S. Haldane, and if it is a success, try parts of the chapter on 'A Day in The Life of a Magician'. It is too long as it stands, but the funniest incidents can be linked into a complete story.

The White Cat

Telling time: 15 minutes.
Audience: Children of 8 upwards.
A straightforward tale for telling.

The Countess D'Aulnoy who wrote this story, lived from 1650 to 1705. She was a witty, clever and beautiful woman whose collections of fairy tales won considerable fame in France. This was a period when sophisticated versions of the old tales gave pleasure at Court and Madame D'Aulnoy's are elaborate compositions that reflect the period admirably. In *The White Cat*, the most appealing of the stories, there are some scraps of folklore, but the author has dressed her characters anew and set them against the luxury of Court life at the close of the seventeenth century.

The stories in their original form would not be read nowadays, but adapted versions are enjoyed by children. In the early nineteenth-century edition from which I have abridged this story, the account of the enchantment of the white Cat is almost as long as the main narrative. As this spoils the effect and deprives the lovers too long of their happy ending, I have cut it drastically. I have omitted the moral also. Such of the colourful details of costume and setting as please children have been retained, and the tale is told with some formality as befits its origin.

The story should be told with gaiety and tenderness, for we become fond of the little white Cat. Keep a feeling of suspense in the scene where the Prince opens nut after nut before finding the five hundred yards of cloth. Full point should be given to the Princess' delicious snub to the King who will not give up his throne. This story is loved by children for its humour and colour and the characters of the little white Cat and her Prince.

A *saraband* is a slow Spanish dance.

The Ballad of Semmerwater

Telling time: 3 minutes.
Audience: Any age.
Occasion: As an introduction to a storytelling programme.

Poetry in a storytelling programme gives variety and pleasure. It can be used as an introduction to a story, or it can tell a story itself. This modern ballad is by a farmer's son from Wharfedale. Semmerwater is a real lake in a deep valley in Wensleydale. Local inhabitants say, 'There's places i' Sommerdell wheer I daresn't go at night', and certainly there is an eerie feeling about the deep, mysterious lake which is the background of this legend.

The poem has an appeal to the ear as well as to the imagination. Children enjoy its rhythm and its telling repetition of 'King's tower and queen's bower.'

Poetry is a very personal thing and every storyteller will have favourite poems he likes to use with children. As a suggestion, try Alfred Noyes' *Ballad of Dick Turpin*, extracts from John Masefield's *Reynard the Fox*, nonsense verse from Edward Lear, poems by Walter de la Mare or Eleanor Farjeon, and modern poems about everyday things. The field is immense and well worth exploration.

The Little Pagan Faun

Telling time: 8 minutes.
Audience: Children of 8 and 9 upwards and adults.
Occasion: Christmas.
An easy story to learn and tell.

Patrick Chalmers wrote this 'fancy' in *Punch* in 1927. Its underlying moral is quite well understood by children. It is told in a musical prose that pleases the ear and is full of pictures that appeal to children. Adults may be dubious of its theology, but, as any child will remind them, this is a *story*.

It may be advisable to tell children before the story begins, what is meant by 'seraphs', those bright pure beings. In this story at least, the 'pagan faun' is as innocent as they are. The difference between 'fawn' and 'faun' should be made plain to children, or they may have a strange picture in their imagination.

Omit for children the latter part of the second paragraph, beginning with the words 'while the faint and tender effulgence . . .' The end of the story needs a little alteration to give a feeling of finality. Omit the first part of the final paragraph so that the last sentences read thus: 'So the little pagan faun trotted off into the woods again, munching his cake and feeling much comforted about things, just as the clocks were striking twelve. It was Christmas Day!'

These last four words can give by their intonation all the wonder and joy that Christmas means to a child.

The Mousewife

Telling time: 18 minutes.
Audience: Children of 10 and 11 upwards and adults.
Occasion: Especially suitable for an audience of women.

An entry in Dorothy Wordsworth's Journal reads as follows:—

'Barbara is an old maid. She had two turtle doves. One of them died, the first year, I think. The other bird continued to live alone in its cage for nine years, but for one whole year it had a companion and daily visitor—a little mouse that used to come and feed with it; and the dove would caress it, and cover it with its wings, and make a loving noise to it. The mouse, though it did not testify equal delight in the dove's company, yet was at perfect ease. The poor mouse disappeared, and the dove was left solitary till its death.'

This is the anecdote that Rumer Godden has taken and transformed into the moving little story of *The Mousewife*. So simply is the story told that the reader is apt to miss the skilful economy of words characteristic of this author's work. The story should be told exactly as it is written, quietly but with warmth. The child will accept it as a story of a mouse and a dove that is lovely to listen to; for the adult it will have an added meaning and poignancy.

For telling, the story should end when the mousewife sees the stars for the first time. ' "And I have seen them for myself," said the mousewife, "without the dove. I can see for myself," said the mousewife, and slowly, proudly, she walked back to bed.' This is the real climax of all that has gone before and no other ending is necessary.

The Hurdy-Gurdy Man

Telling time: 15 minutes.
Audience: Children of 8 upwards.
A reasonably easy story to tell.

A light-hearted story by an American author, Margery Williams Bianco. Her work has a sensitivity and an imaginative quality that gives life to a simple theme.

This is an amusing little story with scope for the storyteller who can convey character—the fat, disagreeable woman at the ham and beef shop, the timid little dressmaker, the teacher who rings the school bell so crossly and the pompous Mayor. If the storyteller can tap out the beat of the magic tune ('Boys and girls come out to play'?), faster and faster as the townspeople join in the dance, it adds life to the story.

Omit the description at the beginning of the story of the town and its people from 'Now it so happened . . .' to 'And so he went his way . . .' Miss Gay gives a similar description when she talks to the hurdy-gurdy man. The Town Clerk need not come into the story at all. The important part of the story comes when the hurdy-gurdy man plays his organ—all else leads up to this and can be pruned a little.

Will modern children know what a hurdy-gurdy is? It might be well to make sure before the story begins.

Lazy Tok

Telling time: 8–10 minutes.
Audience: Children of 7 upwards.
A story that is easy to tell and has the kind of humour that appeals to children.

The story of Lazy Tok, a great favourite with children, comes from a collection of folk tales from Borneo, *The Meeting Pool* by Mervyn Skipper, published in 1929. Each night the animals of the jungle meet at the drinking pool to tell stories. This is the tale told by the Slow Loris who has enormous eyes 'like twin moons floating together under the trees' and is as lazy as Tok herself. He drops asleep almost before he has finished telling the story.

The storyteller should characterise from the very beginning the lively Nipah tree and the lazy drawling Tok. The fat Chinaman and the Booloodoopy should be real people too. The audience never fails to anticipate with delight what is going to happen to Tok, so it is important that the storyteller should not hurry over the climax. It adds to the effect if Tok becomes so lazy that she eats with her eyes shut, for this adds point to the Basket's solemn warning to *look* what he is carrying. When Tok insists that the Basket shall empty itself as usual, there must be a pregnant pause followed by the phrase, 'So the Basket did!' Another short pause will allow the children time to realise what happened then and to shudder with horror and pleasure. The final sentence is more effective as 'As far as I know she is running still—but she is much thinner!'

Unfamiliar words such as 'nipah', 'durian', 'pumelo', 'Booloo-doopy', need not be explained, for children accept them as part of the setting. But for the information of the storyteller, a nipah tree is an East Indian palm, a durian is a large fleshy fruit, a pumelo is a kind of grapefruit, and a Booloodoopy is however you like to imagine him.

The Nightingale

Telling time: 20 minutes.
Audience: Children and adults.
A difficult story to tell.

This is the version used by Marie Shedlock, one of the finest story-tellers this century has known. She was a particularly gifted exponent of Andersen's stories, several of which are included in her book, *The Art of the Storyteller*.

Andersen's stories are not for every audience and not every story-teller feels sympathy for them and can do them justice. They are difficult to tell and Andersen's very individual style does not always translate well into English. After telling *The Nightingale* several times, the storyteller may well find that he is making small altera-tions in some phrases because he feels that these slight adjustments add smoothness and ease to the telling. It is impossible to give firm directions on this—it is an individual matter for the storyteller's ear.

The story should be told simply and smoothly. Enough variety is introduced by the contrasting characters and speech of the stately Emperor, the pompous Lord-in-Waiting, the little kitchen-maid. Probably Andersen meant this tale to be a satire, but his little Nightin-gale has taken over the story and made it into something wise and beautiful and kind.

Because the opening sentence of the story seems silly to some children, it might be better to begin something like this:—

'There was once an Emperor in China who had the most beautiful palace in the world. It was built of the finest porcelain and was so fragile that one hardly dare touch it. In the garden grew wonderful flowers, the most beautiful of which were hung about with silver bells which tinkled when anyone passed by in order to attract attention.'

Where Love Is, God Is

Telling time: 20 minutes.
Audience: Older boys and girls and adults.
Occasion: A Christmas Festival or an occasion on which a story with a religious theme is required.
A difficult story that demands the teller's sincerity and skill.

This is the favourite story of Tolstoy's for telling, although there are others in this collection, *Twenty-Three Tales*, that can be used, *Ivan the Fool* and *A Prisoner in the Caucasus*, for instance.

Where Love Is, God Is is a contemplative story that is moving by its very simplicity. Its construction and its theme make it an effective story to tell.

As the story is a little long for telling, it might be well to summarise the beginning as follows:—

'In a certain town there lived a cobbler, Martin by name. He had a tiny room in a basement, the one window of which looked out on to the street. Through it one could only see the feet of those who passed by, but Martin recognised people by their feet, for there was hardly a pair of boots in the neighbourhood that had not been once or twice through his hands. He had plenty to do for he worked well, used good material, did not charge too much and could be relied upon.

'Martin had always been a good man; but in his old age he began to think more about his soul and to draw nearer to God. His wife and all his children had died and left him alone, and at first Martin had murmured against God because of it. But after a while he realised that his despair came because he was living only for his own happiness and that he must now discover how God wished him to live.

'And so he began to read the Gospels and as he read his heart grew lighter and his life became peaceful and joyful.'

Omit what Martin reads in the sixth chapter of Luke, going straight on to his reading from the seventh chapter, which is the relevant one for this story. Make one more cut when Martin is speaking to Stepánitch (from 'Well you see, I was reading . . .' to 'Blessed are the poor . . .') and replace by one sentence: 'And Martin told Stepánitch his dream and how he had heard the Lord's voice promising to visit him that day.'

The story should be told quietly and with reverence.